WHEN LOVE STRIKES

LOVE ON THE NORTH SHORE BK 6

CHRISTINA TETREAULT

When Love Strikes, ©2019 by Christina Tetreault
Published by Christina Tetreault
Cover Designer: Amanda Walker
Editing: Hot Tree Editing

Digital ISBN: 978-1-7329429-2-9

Print ISBN: 978-1-7329429-3-6

Dear Reader,

Welcome to North Salem, Massachusetts, the setting for this series. Some of you may have visited before, but if not please let me tell you a little about it.

Located forty minutes outside of Boston, it is in a part of the state referred to as the North Shore. North Salem is a close-knit New England town that few people leave. While such camaraderie can be wonderful, especially in times of need, it also means everyone knows each other's business, and squabbles that pop up in high school sometimes continue for years.

Despite the occasional gossip and minor squabbles, North Salem is a wonderful place. I hope you come to love the town and its citizens as much as I do.

Happy Reading,
Christina

PROLOGUE

Not long after moving to town the previous year, Dakota had mapped out four different routes for his weekly runs. Although they all covered three miles, he found varying his runs helped make this particular form of exercise less monotonous. Today's route took him past the town schools and several of the local businesses in North Salem. As he turned onto Grove Street, his mind wasn't on the music coming through his earbuds but the swim he intended to take once he got home. Unfortunately, it'd have to be a quick swim. He wanted to put the second coat of paint on the upstairs bedroom so he could move on to something else.

Dakota waved at Aidan Thomas, a North Salem police officer who was outside mowing his lawn, when he passed by but didn't stop to talk. When a sedan pulled into the driveway of a house farther down the street with a For Sale sign out front, he slowed down. From here he could only see her profile, but the passenger in the car looked like his friend's wife. Sean and Mia had a gorgeous Queen Anne-style home in town, one Sean had spent countless hours renovating. It made little sense for Mia to be looking at another house.

Dakota reached the driveway as both of the car's occupants exited. The moment the passenger turned, he realized his mistake. The woman in the car wasn't Mia but her younger sister, Angie. One afternoon in April, while Sean helped him install the new molding around the windows in a bedroom, he'd mentioned Angie was looking to buy a house in town. If Angie and a real estate agent were here, this must be one she was considering.

"Dakota, hi." She waved and smiled as he approached the car. "How have you been?"

He'd last seen her in early May. He'd gone over to shoot pool with Sean and Tony, and she'd been there. Whenever Angie visited, she stayed with her sister and brother-in-law. And since Mia and Sean's wedding the previous fall, her visits had become more and more frequent. According to Sean, she'd decided it would be better if she had a place of her own in North Salem so she didn't need to intrude on them.

In his opinion, buying a house so she had a place to stay when she visited was extravagant. There was a bed-and-breakfast in town, not to mention plenty of hotels within a half-hour drive of North Salem. If either Sean or his wife shared his opinion, neither ever said.

"Good. You?" She looked amazing. Then again, she did every time he saw her. More importantly, she was always friendly despite her celebrity status.

"Busy, but good. We've been looking at houses all morning, and we have a few more after this one."

If it had been in his budget when he'd been looking at homes, he would've added this one to his list even though it was much larger than he needed. Even the house he owned was bigger than a single guy needed.

"Will you be in town much longer?" They knew each other well enough to talk like they were now, but he wouldn't mind getting to know her better. If she stayed in North Salem until Mia had the baby, he might be able to do that.

Angie frowned as she shook her head. "I wish I could be. I'd love to be here when Mia has the baby. But I'm flying out to Italy on Monday, and I'll be there for about a month finishing up a movie."

Considering she was off to Italy, a place he'd love to visit again, she didn't sound very excited. Of course, she was going for work not pleasure. Twice he'd traveled to Hawaii and Puerto Rico, once for work and once on a vacation. Somehow being there for work had diminished his enjoyment of the areas despite the beautiful locations.

The real estate agent cleared her throat, a sign she was eager to get going.

"Have a safe trip. I'll see you later."

ANGIE WATCHED Dakota until he turned the corner. If she didn't have several more houses to look at after this one, she would've asked him to meet her for a coffee later. She'd noticed him at her sister's wedding. Thanks to his incredible smile and something she couldn't put her finger on, Dakota stood out in a crowd. Between the short interactions she'd had with him and what her sister told her about him, he came across as a nice man, and it'd been a long time since she had a nice guy in her life. Unfortunately, she couldn't pursue a relationship with Dakota or anyone else in town right now. Next week the studio expected her on the set in Rome, and she'd be there until well into the summer.

No longer able to admire Dakota's retreating form, she turned toward Olivia. She'd reached out to the local real estate agent in early April after deciding it was time to get a place near her sister. Over the past couple months, she'd looked at several homes and even talked to a local contractor about building one in the new development located off Blueberry Court. Except for one, each had been beautiful, and any of them would've sufficed. But none had felt right. She couldn't explain it, and she'd certainly tried. Deep down, she knew when she found the right house, she'd know.

"As you can see, the house was built in 1820, and it is listed with the National Register of Historic Places." Olivia pointed toward the plaque on the front of the house. "The property has been on the market for almost a year, and the owners are eager to sell. They've already purchased a place in Florida."

Olivia unlocked the front door and preceded her inside. "On this level, there are five rooms and a half bath. Upstairs you will find four bedrooms. The master has its own bathroom while the other three share one. There are also two small rooms in the attic and another small bathroom."

She'd read over the information regarding the house last night and checked out the pictures included in the listing, so she had a good idea of what to expect when she walked inside. What she wasn't expecting was the little voice in her head telling her this was the one before she even stepped in a single room.

The pictures on the internet didn't do the place justice. They didn't pick up the tiny details throughout the home, the type of details that rarely showed up in houses built today. The only two drawbacks she found as she walked through were the lack of showers and the dreadful kitchen, but an interior designer could correct both areas and a few other little things she'd like to see changed.

Angie followed the real estate agent back down the stairs leading up to the attic. The rooms up there were not even half the size of the other bedrooms, and she couldn't imagine using one as a bedroom herself. Forget about the bathroom. A person could sit on the toilet and brush their teeth at the same time, the room was so small. "I think this might be the one."

"Do you still want to look at the other houses on the list?"

"It doesn't hurt to look." They had the time, so they might as well. However, she didn't expect any of them would feel as right as this one.

ONE

Six Weeks Later

THE CLOSER DAKOTA SMITH got to town, the more at
ease he became. No matter the type of day he'd had at work,
this happened every time he returned home at night. It was
the main reason he'd moved to North Salem after living just
outside of Boston for two years. Tonight, more than any other
night in recent months, he needed the peace being in town
always brought him.

He'd been an FBI agent for almost seven years, first in
Albany and now in Boston, and he'd seen a lot of things—
things most people didn't even want to witness in their night-
mares. Regardless, some people and situations still kicked
him in the ass. The combined search and arrest warrant he'd
helped execute today had done just that. Even now as he
headed down Main Street, he wished he could scrub away the
memories of what he'd seen, the same way he'd washed away
the smell of cigarette smoke from his body when he got back
to the office.

After turning onto Fender Drive, Dakota took a right into the parking lot for Peggy Sue's Café. He'd been up since three this morning, and the adrenaline rush he always experienced before and during an arrest had long since evaporated. If he had any hope of making it past seven tonight, he needed a double espresso. Any other night he wouldn't care about staying awake. He lived alone. No one cared what time he called it a night or got up in the morning. Unfortunately, hitting the hay the moment he walked into the house tonight wasn't an option.

Long before he'd known about today's big arrest, he'd agreed to host this month's poker game. He'd attended several games since his move to town, but this evening's would be the first time he'd hosted one. Even if it weren't the first time, the game was at his house; he wouldn't want to cancel on everyone at the last minute.

The scent of coffee and fresh baked goods hit Dakota the moment he walked inside the popular coffee shop. Regardless of the time, Peggy Sue's was rarely empty. Tonight was no different. Although approaching dinnertime, most of the tables inside were occupied, and a short line of customers stood at the counter waiting to place their orders.

"Dakota, I haven't seen you in weeks. How are you?" Mrs. Mitchell inquired as he approached her table.

If he had to guess, he'd say the friendly widow was in her early nineties. Despite her advanced age, she still lived alone. Actually, her house was only down the street from him. And when she wasn't spending time at the senior center doing yoga or reading to young children at the library, she was keeping up to date on all the town news and gossip. If a person wanted to know what was going on, all they needed to do was talk to Mrs. Mitchell.

He didn't have a lot of time to waste, but not stopping to talk with the older woman was impossible. Something about her grandmotherly personality made even the grumpiest person in town stop and chat with her, no matter how much of a rush they were in.

"You haven't been sick, have you? My friend's grandchildren were both diagnosed with bronchitis last week. I couldn't believe it when she told me. Apparently, several children at their summer camp have it," she continued, making it impossible for him to answer her previous question.

"I'm fine, just busy. How are you?"

Inquiring into Mrs. Mitchell's well-being could be a dangerous endeavor, a fact he'd learned the hard way during an encounter while grocery shopping. Instead of getting a short two- or three-sentence answer, he'd ended up standing in the bread aisle with her for close to half an hour. Hopefully, today she'd give him the condensed version of whatever was on her mind so he could get going.

"Wonderful. My granddaughter is moving in with me in about another week. She accepted a new position in Boston and is going to live with me for the foreseeable future. Even with the increase in salary, she hasn't been able to find anything affordable closer to the city."

He understood that well. Although not the most expensive city in the country, the housing costs in and around Boston were high. When he'd transferred from the office in Albany to the one in Boston three years ago, he'd lived in a one-bedroom apartment, and his rent each month equaled what he was now paying for a mortgage on a three-bedroom home with half an acre of land. Not to mention his monthly rent hadn't included the fee he'd paid to park his car and motorcycle.

"You must be looking forward to having the company." Between work and friends, he didn't spend a lot of time alone. Despite the fact that Mrs. Mitchell kept herself busy during the day, he imagined she got lonely at night. And as far as he'd seen, she rarely went out in the evening. At least every time he drove by her home, her car was in the driveway and the lights were on inside.

Mrs. Mitchell nodded and reached for her purse hanging over the back of her chair. "When Trisha gets settled, you'll have to stop by and meet her. She's around your age." After searching around in her purse, she pulled out her cell phone. "This is us on Memorial Day."

She held the phone toward Dakota, leaving him no other option than to accept the device.

He glanced at the picture of the smiling women. Despite the age difference between Mrs. Mitchell and her grand-daughter, there was no missing the family resemblance.

Before he replied, he considered his words. Telling the woman her granddaughter was pretty wouldn't be a lie, because she was. At the same time, Mrs. Mitchell's previous comments gave him the impression she was thinking about setting him up with her granddaughter. Although not opposed to having a special woman in his life, he didn't want someone fixing him up. He'd let his mom do it once, and it had turned into a major headache.

Dakota handed back the device. "It's a great picture of the two of you."

"I had it made into an eight-by-ten so I could frame it." She deposited the cell phone back into her purse.

He stayed and chatted with the woman for a few more minutes before joining the line at the counter and getting the double espresso he desperately needed.

An hour and a half later, Dakota was in the process of paying the delivery guy for the pizzas when Mack and his wife pulled into his driveway. Since they lived just up the street from him, across from St. Mark's Church, Mack usually walked over when he visited. And he'd spent plenty of time at the house helping with renovations. If it hadn't been for Mack and the other friends he'd made since moving to town, the house would still be the wreck he'd walked into almost a year ago, having made the mistake of buying a fore-closed home without seeing the inside—a mistake Dakota would never make again. Tonight it made sense that Mack and Jessie drove over despite the short distance between their homes. Jessie was pregnant with twins, and while he didn't remember her exact due date, he knew it was in about another three weeks.

"Thanks for hosting tonight," Jessie said, entering the house.

It'd been about a week and a half since he'd last seen her, but his friend's wife looked like she'd doubled in size since then.

"Grace and I made double chocolate chip brownies this afternoon." She held up a plastic container. "She insisted we make two batches so she could take some to her sleepover tonight at her cousin's and we could bring some here."

Anyone who'd ever seen Grace and Jessie together would assume they were mother and daughter. Jessie treated Grace as if she was her biological child rather than her stepdaughter. And Grace gave no indication that she thought of Jessie as anything other than another mom. He'd never seen Grace interact with her birth mother, but according to Mack, Grace and Jessie bond's was far stronger than the one the young girl had with his ex-wife.

"Tell her I said thank you." He put the container on top of the pizza boxes. "Make yourself at home."

And please sit down. Just looking at her standing there was making his feet hurt. In the few years he'd known Jessie, he'd never heard her complain, but the poor woman had to be incredibly uncomfortable. Sitting down might not make it any better for her, but at least he'd feel better.

Not long after Jessie and Mack's arrival, Tony and his

wife walked in. Less than a minute later, Striker and his fiancée rang the doorbell. Of the three men, Dakota had spent the least amount of time with Striker. However, even Striker had helped a few times on the numerous projects the house had required.

Tony's wife, Cat, added a takeout container to the collection of food already on the extra folding table he'd set out. "Sorry, I didn't have time to cook, so we grabbed some buffalo wings and tenders from Masterson's on the way over."

It was an unspoken rule that everyone contributed to the food available at the monthly poker games. He'd expected Cat to bring the homemade guacamole and chips she usually brought and he always enjoyed. He wouldn't complain about her offering though. While not the only restaurant in town, Masterson's was the largest and perhaps the oldest in North Salem, and it served the best buffalo wings and tenders he'd ever eaten.

"Kelsey sent me a message. She and Drew are running about thirty minutes late. She said to start without them," Cat continued as she added two slices of pizza to her plate.

After setting down his plate piled high with a little of everything, Dakota shuffled the cards while the rest of his guests took their seats around the table. Before he could deal a single card, the doorbell rang again. Other than Drew and Kelsey, the only other people who regularly joined their games were Sean and his wife. He wasn't expecting them tonight. Sean hadn't said it, but he didn't expect to see them at a game again until maybe after Halloween. Since June, when their daughter was born, they'd made few outings, and neither wanted to leave their daughter with anyone, not even family members.

"Mind if I join you?" Sean asked when Dakota answered the door.

"Since it looks like you brought something from Peggy Sue's, you can come in." He stepped back so Sean could enter. "All alone tonight?"

Sean nodded and made a pit stop to add the pastry box to the food spread. Then he grabbed a plate. "Mia's at home with Natalie, waiting for Angie. Her plane landed about an hour ago."

An image of Mia's younger sister popped up in his mind. She was almost identical to Sean's wife, and *Today Magazine* had voted Angelina Troy the world's sexiest woman earlier in the year—a title Mia herself had earned as well before meeting Sean and leaving Hollywood behind.

Dakota retook his seat and picked up the deck of cards. "Is she alone, or is your mother-in-law with her?"

It was no secret that Sean and his mother-in-law didn't get along. Dakota had no idea of the relationship between Sean and his father-in-law, but he'd never heard Sean complain about the man.

"Alone. The wicked witch isn't supposed to be back until October." Sean dropped into a seat between Tony and Striker. "Mia is trying to convince her to stay at the Victorian Rose when she comes instead of with us like she did on her last visit, so she'll still be close. If Lynn has to visit, I'd rather she stays in Boston."

The Victorian Rose was the town's only bed-and-breakfast and conveniently located next door to Sean and Mia.

"So far she hasn't had any luck. Lynn has a one-track mind and doesn't like to listen to anyone's suggestions," Sean grumbled before sinking his teeth into a buffalo wing.

Tony clapped Sean on the shoulder. "We've got a spare bedroom. It's yours if you want it when your mother-in-law arrives."

"There's a decent chance I'll take you up on that offer, Tony."

Nine out of ten times, talk of his mother-in-law put Sean in a foul mood. Not that Dakota blamed the guy, considering the stories his friend had shared about the way she treated him. Picking up the cards again, he started to deal. "How long is your sister-in-law staying with you?"

"She's only staying with us tonight. Tomorrow she's moving into her house."

Two weeks ago, they'd been installing the hardwood floor in one of the upstairs bedrooms when Sean mentioned his wife had acted on Angie's behalf and signed the closing paperwork on the old Federalist-style home she'd purchased. At the time, he said she'd also hired some hotshot interior design firm out of Boston to come in and revamp the entire home, even though according to Sean it wasn't necessary. Unless the team they'd brought in had worked around the clock, he didn't think they could have finished by now.

"Did she change her mind about the remodel?" Tony's question echoed Dakota's thoughts.

Sean checked the cards in his hand. "No, but she decided to move in anyway. Mia thinks she'll be staying in town for four or five months, but I disagree. I think she'll get bored and head back to California before Halloween."

Some people might have made a similar prediction about Sean's wife. Yet she'd been living in town for a few years and, despite her mom's best efforts, showed no signs of leaving North Salem or her husband—two things Lynn Troy regularly suggested Mia do.

"She might surprise you." Jessie added her two cents to the conversation before reaching for the brownie on her plate.

"As long as it doesn't mean Lynn is around more, I hope she does stick around. Mia's closer to Angie than to her older sister. And I know she misses her."

Living far apart from family could be tough. Dakota knew it firsthand. He hadn't seen his older sister in over a year. It'd been even longer since he saw his older brother. He hadn't even seen his parents in close to eight months. Phone calls and text messages were nice, but they were both poor substitutes for actual visits.

ANGIE APPLIED the brakes as she approached the stopped traffic. Until this moment, her day had proceeded like a perfectly executed movie scene. She'd made it through the airport and onto her flight out of LAX without a single person recognizing her. She'd thought the TSA agent might when she handed over her boarding pass and ID, but the man gave no indication he did. Perhaps he'd assumed if she was *that* Angelina Troy, she would fly on a private jet, something she sometimes wished she owned, instead of a commercial one along with everyone else. Whatever the reason, he'd handed her back the papers without even a smile and then called the next person in line forward. Even the flight from Los Angeles to Boston had been a pleasant one, free of any turbulence.

Once she'd landed in Boston, she pulled her baseball hat back on and made it from the gate through the airport and out to her rental car with only a single minor incident. Unlike the TSA agent in California, after she handed over her driver's license at the rental car agency, the thirtysomething woman working there did ask if she was the Angelia Troy who'd stared in *Deceptive Desire,* which had been released around Valentine's Day. For a heartbeat or two, she'd toyed with the idea of lying and telling her that, no, she wasn't the actress in question but merely shared a name with her. She hadn't, though, and the woman had all but jumped over the counter with excitement. Thankfully the employee kept her voice low when she'd gone on to tell Angie how much she loved her in both *Deceptive Desire* and

A Prince to Call Her Own, so no one else paid them any attention.

She hadn't expected her travel today to be so easy. For the past few years now, it seemed everywhere she went, people either recognized her or there were some paparazzi waiting in the shadows to catch a picture of her buying lunch. Then again, she rarely went out of her way to disguise herself when she went out. She loved fashion and never left her house dressed like she was today. And the only time she wore her hair pulled back in a ponytail and went makeup-free was when she either exercised or if a movie role called for it. This morning, though, she'd taken her sister Mia's advice and dressed in a pair of shorts and a blue-and-white-striped T-shirt. She'd skipped all makeup except for some mascara and tied her hair up in a simple ponytail.

In the future, when Angie wanted to travel and keep a low profile, she'd be sure to duplicate today's look. Although she didn't plan on doing any travel again soon, no matter how much her mom and Avery, her eldest sister and personal assistant, pressured her to reconsider her decision.

The line of traffic moved, and Angie pressed down on the accelerator. Up ahead she could see the North Salem exit, and she switched off the car's GPS. She probably could've made it this far even without it, but she'd turned it on just to be on the safe side. Angie definitely wouldn't need it in town. She'd driven through much of North Salem, looking at homes back in the spring with her sister as well as with the real estate agent, so she knew her way around almost as well as Mia, who'd been living there since before she married the previous year.

Tapping her fingers against the steering wheel in rhythm with the song blasting from the speakers, Angie passed the town common. At present it was empty, but it wasn't so dark yet that she couldn't make out the playground located in one corner and the large bandstand at the opposite end. According to Mia and her husband, the town common was an active place. Regardless of the month, children enjoyed the playground, and when it snowed they liked to build snowmen. Once a month, starting in the late spring and ending in early August, the town held a block party on the common. As crazy as it might seem to some of her friends, she was eager to attend one before they ended for the year. From Mia's descriptions, they sounded like nothing she'd ever experienced before. Thanks to her sister, she also knew it wasn't uncommon for everyone, from the North Salem High School band to local country singers, to perform on the bandstand during the nicer months of the year.

A giant raindrop hit the windshield. Dark clouds stopped her from putting down the convertible's top before she left the rental car parking lot, but until now a single drop of water hadn't fallen. She'd hoped to make it to Mia's house before the rain started, but it looked like she'd used up all of her good luck today. On her twenty-first birthday, she'd hydroplaned and hit a stone wall on her way back to campus. Although she had suffered nothing worse than a concussion and a broken wrist, she'd hated driving in the rain ever since, regardless of whether it was nine in the morning or nine at night.

Like all the other times she'd visited town, a No Vacancy sign hung outside the Victorian Rose, which was owned by Sean and his mom. Her sister had met her husband when she'd stayed there before starting work on what had turned out to be her final movie. While their mom continuously insisted Mia had made the biggest mistake of her life by giving up her career and marrying Sean, Mia appeared happy. In Angie's opinion, her sister's happiness was all that mattered. Of course, Mom disagreed, so she avoided discussing Mia's life choices with her. Unfortunately, sometimes it was impossible.

The motion sensor lights on the garage switched on as soon as Angie pulled into the driveway. Even before she made it up the walkway, the front door of the historic home opened. While Mia remained in the house and out of the rain, the family's large Irish wolfhound, Max, bounded down the steps to greet her. She'd quickly learned the giant dog was a big softy, but anyone seeing him for the first time would probably take a step or two back.

Max didn't make a sound as he approached and stopped by her side. "Hey, Max." Angie paused and scratched the dog near his ears. When she started walking again, Max fell into step alongside her and stayed there until they reached the door.

Her sister barely let her enter the house before hugging her. "I expected you sooner. Did your plane arrive late?"

"There was an accident on the highway." Angie moved out of her sister's embrace and listened for any sound. Considering Mia had a husband and a newborn in the house, it was quiet. "Not that I'm not happy to see you, but where's Natalie?"

Born in June, Natalie was her only niece. She'd hoped to visit right after her birth, but work on her last film had made leaving Rome, where she'd been at the time, impossible until a week ago.

"I put Natalie in her bassinet when I saw you pull in." Mia closed the door and nodded toward the living room off the main foyer.

"Let me guess, Sean is standing guard next to it."

When she'd first met her brother-in-law, she'd been more than a little surprised. She'd always assumed Mia would end up with someone like Brad St. Pierre, a fellow actor she'd dated on and off for years. After all, until Mia met Sean, she'd dated big-name actors and professional athletes. She'd even been with a musician for several months. Sean, on the other hand, was an extremely intelligent, no-nonsense kind of guy who put his family's needs before his own wants and desires. Even though they'd seemed like a mismatched pair in the beginning, Sean adored her sister and made Mia happier than Angie remembered her being since they were kids and still living a few streets over from their grandparents. And Angie loved him for it, unlike Mom, who'd decided even before she met Sean to dislike him and had never changed her mind.

Mia shook her head slightly. "He finally stopped doing that two weeks ago."

Truthfully, Angie wasn't sure if Mia was joking or not. Mia had told her how protective he was of his much younger half sister, Taylor. She could only imagine how protective he'd be of his only daughter.

"I can't tell if you're pulling my leg or not."

Angie followed Mia into the living room. Unlike the main living room she'd walked through in her house this morning before leaving for the airport, this one was warm and inviting. A few pictures from Sean and Mia's wedding hung on the wall. There were also pictures of Mia and Sean's nephew, Garrett, up there. A colorful area rug covered the floor, and a throw blanket hung over the back of the sofa.

"He's never stood guard, but I have caught him just watching her more times than I can count."

A pastel-colored bassinet was against the wall close to the window seat, and Angie made a beeline for it. She wasn't the only one. Max walked past her and immediately stationed himself on the floor near it, as if to guard Natalie from any possible threats. She wondered how long it'd taken her brother-in-law to teach the dog to do that.

"Where is Sean anyway?"

"He isn't here. I strongly suggested he go to the poker game tonight so we could have some time alone. I feel like I haven't talked to you in years."

The most perfect baby girl looked back up at Angie from the bassinet, wearing a one-piece footed outfit with pink poodles on it. Natalie's hair was a few shades lighter than Mia's, and at least for the moment, her eyes were a unique bluish green. Since Mia's eyes were more of a whiskey color, the same shade as hers, and Sean's were green, what color Natalie's would finally be was anyone's guess.

Her first instinct was to pick up her niece, but she held off. "Can I pick her up?"

"Of course."

She didn't need to hear anything else. Reaching down, Angie picked up Natalie while Max kept a watchful eye on her every move. "Never mind about Sean standing guard. Max seems to be doing a good job of it himself. How long did it take Sean to teach him to sit here like this?"

"Sean didn't teach him anything. Max has kept a close eye on Natalie since the day we brought her home from the hospital. Are you hungry?"

Angie glanced briefly at her sister. "Starving." Airplane food in first class might be better than the meals served in the coach section, but it still left a lot to be desired.

"I made baked stuffed shrimp for dinner. If you want, I can heat you up some."

Her head flew up. "You made baked stuffed shrimp? As in you moved it from the freezer to the oven, or as in you bought the ingredients and followed a recipe?"

Before Mia hit it big and their parents moved them to California, they'd both spent hours baking cookies with their grandmother. However, neither had ever cooked meals with her or their mother for that matter. Once they relocated, staff working at the house had prepared all their meals, making cooking lessons with Mom impossible.

"It's homemade." Mia started to walk away. "But if you'd rather have a sandwich, I can make you one."

Angie followed her sister out of the room and toward the kitchen. "I definitely want the shrimp. I knew you'd gotten the hang of the basics, but it seems like a big jump to go from making a meatloaf to baked stuffed shrimp."

"Maureen stepped up her cooking lessons around Valentine's Day. Last week she showed me how to make homemade ravioli."

"Maybe I should ask your mother-in-law to give me a few lessons."

While living in North Salem, she'd need to eat. There were enough restaurants in town that she could pick up takeout occasionally, but doing so every night would get old fast. That left her with two options: cook her own meals or hire someone to come in and do it. She didn't know everyone in town, but she doubted anyone had an individual come in to prepare their meals.

Mia pulled a large covered container from the refrigerator and added a generous helping to a plate before popping it into the microwave. "Next time Maureen comes over, join us. She won't mind an extra person in the kitchen."

"Maybe I will." She pulled out a chair and sat. "Who hosted tonight's game, anyway?"

She'd never been around for any of them, but Angie knew the monthly event, which had started a couple of years ago, moved from house to house. Judging by the way Mia talked about it, the evening was less about playing cards and more about sitting down with good friends and enjoying each other's company while eating a lot of food that wasn't all that nutritious. Although she'd never played poker, not even a computer version on her cell phone, she planned to ask Mia and Sean if she could attend the next time it was their turn to host. Much like the block parties held in town, the monthly poker game was unlike anything she usually experienced, and for the past several months she'd grown bored—no, that wasn't quite right. She'd grown *weary* of her present lifestyle. She needed a change. Moving to North Salem and closer to her sister and niece were the first steps to making that change. And, while here, she'd finally make up her mind about some of the other changes she was considering.

"The game was at Dakota's house tonight." Mia added two glasses of iced tea to the table.

Between her sister's wedding and visits to town since Mia moved there, she'd met several of Mia and Sean's friends. Dakota she'd only been around perhaps half a dozen times, yet she had no trouble recalling the man in question. By Hollywood's current standards, he'd be just another average Joe. He didn't possess the look needed to land the leading role in a summer blockbuster or appear on the cover of every magazine out there.

But he had a killer smile.

When Sean introduced her to Dakota and he'd smiled at her, it'd taken her a second or two longer than necessary to form a proper response—an experience she couldn't recall happening since she'd been fifteen and met Christian Peck, who'd been costarring in a movie with Mia. Even when she'd run into Dakota briefly while looking at houses one after-noon, and he'd offered up a smile and a greeting, she'd found herself off-kilter.

Mia set a dish down in front of her. The mere aroma made Angie's mouth water.

"Do you want me to hold her while you eat?"

Angie glanced at the steaming dish and then at her niece. "No, but it's probably a good idea." She handed over Natalie and then picked up her fork. Even though Maureen had been giving her sister cooking lessons for a while now, Angie took only a small forkful of food. A mixture of shrimp, clams, scallops, and a few other flavors she couldn't put her finger on melted in her mouth. "Wow, this is good. I'm impressed."

"My mother-in-law is a good teacher. You should have tasted the homemade pasta sauce I made right before Natalie was born. It was almost as good as the one Gram makes."

While Mia filled her in on some of the other recipes she'd conquered thanks to her mother-in-law's cooking lessons, Angie listened and ate. In truth, her mind kept wandering away from her sister's new skills in the kitchen and to a certain North Salem resident whose smile was capable of leaving most women temporarily speechless.

"Is Dakota a permanent part of the poker group?" Sometime last winter Mia mentioned Dakota had joined them for a game. If he was the host of tonight's little get-together, maybe he had become a regular participant.

With a nod, Mia repositioned Natalie and then reached for her glass of iced tea. "I don't think he's missed one since March."

"When is it going to be your turn to host again?"

"Probably not until sometime in the fall."

Waiting until the fall to see if Dakota's smile still managed to momentarily clear her head of all thoughts didn't work for her.

"Why? Do you want to come?"

"As long as no one else will mind." And while she waited for the next poker game at Sean and Mia's house, she'd keep her eyes peeled for Dakota and his mind-clearing smile.

TWO

MIA HANDED Angie a coffee mug before setting one down on the table for Sean, who'd taken Natalie upstairs to change her diaper. "What time is the furniture being delivered?"

Thanks to the internet, she'd been able to order furniture and schedule its delivery last week, even though she'd been on the other side of the country until yesterday. She really didn't know how people managed before they invented the internet and online shopping. Despite a strong desire to order enough furniture to fill the house, she'd purchased only the absolute minimum since they hadn't started the renovations she wanted.

"They said between ten and one."

"Are you positive you don't want to stay with us? Living in a house while it's being renovated can be a huge headache. We've got the room, and Sean doesn't mind."

Although Sean had done most of the renovations on the home before Mia moved in, she'd been around when he started.

"I think I'll be okay. But if it starts to get to me, I'll let you know."

"Do you know when they're going to start the work?"

Angie pulled a poppy seed bagel out of the package and covered it with cream cheese before adding it to her plate. Most mornings she ended up with one of those meal replacement shakes Jillian, her personal trainer and nutritionist, insisted upon. The woman wasn't here, and Angie didn't plan on seeing her in the near future, so today she'd enjoy all the cream cheese and carbs she wanted.

"Not a clue. Later today I'm meeting with Gregg so we can review his most recent designs."

She'd hired Ducat and Wakefield Designers, an interior design firm out of Boston, because they were supposedly the best around. So far Gregg, the interior designer assigned to the project, had not produced a single design she liked despite the numerous phone calls and emails they'd exchanged.

"What was wrong with the last ones?"

Angie cut into the omelet her sister had prepared and considered the question. Overall, the designs Gregg emailed her had been gorgeous, worthy of any interior design magazine or website. But they hadn't been right for a house built in 1820, or her for that matter. Or at least not the present her. Two or three years ago, when she'd been remodeling her first house, she would've approved them with only a few minor changes.

"They were too modern for the house. And they were, I don't know, cold maybe. If I'd approved them, the place would've had the same feel as my house in Los Angeles."

"I'm a little confused. Didn't you have the house redone after you bought it?"

She nodded. "Those designs fit the overall style of the house, and for the most part, I liked them. But even when it was being finished, there were a few details Mom strongly influenced. Actually, I'm thinking about selling it and maybe building something new if I go back to California."

Mia's hand paused on the way to her coffee mug. "If you go back? Are you thinking about staying in North Salem permanently?"

Hope resonated in her sister's voice. Only about two years apart in age, they'd always been close. When they'd both lived on the West Coast, they'd spent much of their free time together, doing everything from exercising to shopping. It'd been a difficult adjustment when Mia moved back to New England to be with Sean. And as much as Angie adored her brother-in-law, in the beginning she'd resented him a little for the distance separating her and Mia.

"Maybe. I haven't decided, but I'm leaning in that direction. Mom and Avery keep hopping on the fact that I'm thinking about not returning to Los Angeles. They think I should visit for a month or so, get North Salem out of my system, and come home. I never should've mentioned to either of them that I was even considering a permanent move. You know how they get."

"How who gets?" Sean once again joined them in the kitchen.

A move wasn't the only thing she was leaning toward. She'd discuss those thoughts with Mia when they were alone, because there were a few questions she wanted to ask her sister—questions she didn't want to ask in front of Sean, such as whether or not Mia ever regretted giving up her acting career. Nothing Mia ever said or did gave her any reason to think she regretted leaving Hollywood behind, but that didn't mean she didn't from time to time.

Mia took Natalie from Sean so he could get started on his breakfast. "Mom and Avery."

The muscle in Sean's jaw twitched, but otherwise he didn't comment. Instead, he sat and reached for his fork. "You're welcome to stay with us while they work on the house."

"Already offered, and she refused."

"Don't worry, I'll be here so much to see Natalie it'll be like I'm living here anyway."

Leaving Natalie after breakfast was no easy task. She'd already missed the first several weeks of the little girl's life and didn't want to miss any more. Mia's invitation to come back and join them later for dinner helped her finally get out the door.

Rather than take the most direct route from her sister's house to Grove Street, she drove down by the Stonefield Dam, a part of town she hadn't explored yet, and the park the town had set up following a hurricane a few years earlier. Mia had mentioned a bike trail started in the park and continued into Marblehead. Although she'd never walked the entire thing, Mia said she sometimes took Natalie for a walk along part of the trail in her stroller. Before winter rolled in, Angie wanted to take a bike ride along it. She couldn't recall the last time she'd sat on a bike that wasn't inside a gym. Of course, that meant she'd have to first buy a bicycle. Thanks to her computer, she could do that without leaving her house.

When Angie stepped out of her car, puddles filled the driveway from the previous night's rainstorm. She avoided the small moat that had formed in the front walkway by walking over the soggy lawn instead. Unlike the house, which the previous owners had kept in excellent condition—even if it was outdated—the driveway and front walkway were a disaster. Both sagged in some areas, collecting rain, and there were entire sections missing. But next week both the walkway and the driveway were being replaced, and her makeshift moat would be a thing of the past.

Once around the water, she stepped back on the path and paused to look at the structure. The day she checked out the place, it had called to her. Even before she examined a single room, she'd known this was the house she'd been looking for.

Unlike the other homes on the street, hers was built almost entirely of brick. Four large chimneys extended toward the sky, and the front door was positioned in the center of the first floor. A portico held up by two large white pillars extended over the front steps, and a fan-shaped window over the door along with two glass window panels allowed sunlight into the front foyer and hall. Attached to the front of the home was a national registry plaque stating the year the home was built and by whom. She hadn't looked into it, but she suspected this was among the oldest homes still being used in town.

Unlocking the front door, Angie stepped into the front foyer. An unexpected sense of excitement stopped her short. She had no idea why, but she felt as if she was about to start on something new and exhilarating. Although not exactly the same, the sensation was similar to what she used to experience when she started work on a new movie.

Back in June, when she'd gone through the house, a runner had covered the stairs leading up to the second floor. With it gone, the wear and tear of almost two centuries of footsteps was clear to see. Who had gone up and down the stairs? Had the original owner been a prominent politician in Massachusetts, or had he been a successful merchant? What about children? How many children had run up and down the stairs? For perhaps the first time, Angie understood why her sister loved history so much.

She hadn't been inside since the day she put in the offer on the house. Mia, to whom she'd given power of attorney, had done the final walk-through with the real estate agent before signing the necessary paperwork the day of the closing. She'd also brought the interior designer through the house so he could take measurements and see what he was starting with.

This morning, Angie was eager to see the entire home

again. The room on her right seemed as good a place to start as any.

A large fireplace, just one of many in the house, took up much of one wall. Built-in bookcases flanked it on either side, but otherwise the room was empty, making it appear much larger than she remembered. Slightly faded period-appropriate wallpaper covered the walls. One of the previous owners, an attorney, had used the room as a home office. Since she had no need of an office, she imagined turning this room into a small library. She could picture herself curled up near the fireplace, reading a book while it snowed outside.

Slowly she made her way through each of the other rooms on the first floor. Rather than fill the house with twenty-first-century furniture, the previous owners had decorated the rooms with antique pieces. With all of it gone, it was easy to spot the various minor repairs the house needed, not that it really surprised her. The house was almost two hundred years old.

Unlike in many of the other rooms, there was no wallpaper covering the walls in the kitchen. Judging by the cabinets and countertops, someone had remodeled the room in the early 1980s. The walls were a bright cheery yellow that seemed out of place in the home because everywhere else, the owners had used colors more in line with those found in the early nineteenth century.

At some point, the entire room would need to be gutted and redone, but it wasn't number one on her list of priorities. The master bath needed updating first. She could live with an old stove and dated cabinets, but she needed a shower; the house only had bathtubs, and she wanted her Jacuzzi.

A narrower and less decorative staircase led from the kitchen to the second floor. She knew enough about older homes to know the staff of the original owners of the house would have used this staircase

Much like most of the rooms on the first floor, all the bedrooms contained fireplaces, and they were all functional according to the listing agent. While she might use some of the ones downstairs—the idea of a fire burning on a cold winter night was appealing—she wasn't sure she'd ever use the ones on the second floor, since it would mean she'd have to lug wood upstairs. When she met with Gregg today, she wanted to ask him about the possibility of having a gas insert added to at least the fireplace in the master bedroom—an idea that hadn't occurred to her until Sean mentioned it last night.

Upstairs, Angie entered the second largest of the four bedrooms. Narrow built-in bookcases flanked both sides of the fireplace in the room; however, the builders had added none to the other bedrooms. Although empty now, when she was here in June, the room had contained a large canopy bed complete with bed curtains. The curtains, which still hung over the windows, had matched those on the bed. Maybe she should've asked the previous owners if they wanted to sell the bed rather than move it. It had fit the room perfectly.

"Too late now."

Turning away toward the doorway, she was about to walk out when she noticed one of the bookcases stood out a bit.

"It's your imagination. Built-in bookcases don't move. It's probably a shadow."

Despite her one-sided argument, she walked closer to the fireplace. No question about it, the bookcase to the right of the mantel was no longer flush against the wall like its counterpart to the left.

Maybe she was wrong and these weren't built in like the ones downstairs. Grabbing one of the empty shelves with two hands, she gently pulled, expecting to find a nice flat wall behind the piece of furniture. Instead she found a ladder leading up. She didn't stop to think before she climbed it.

Angie found herself in a windowless room that had to be

in the attic. The ceiling was low, almost too low for her to stand up straight, and she doubted she'd be able to stretch out completely on the floor.

Pulling her cell phone out of her pocket, she hit Mia's contact information. When her sister answered, she didn't give her a chance to even say hello. "Can you come over?"

She wasn't as big a history buff as her sister, although she enjoyed learning about it a great deal, but her instincts were telling her the hidden passage she'd just uncovered had been part of the Underground Railroad. If anyone would want to see the room, it was Mia.

"We're on our way to see Sean's dad and sister, but if it's an emergency, we can turn around."

"No emergency."

"Are you sure?"

"Positive. I just wanted to show you something I found. I'll tell you about it tonight."

DAKOTA FLIPPED the switch on the wall and, as he expected, nothing happened. The night before, he'd met some friends in Boston for the baseball game against Baltimore, followed by a drink and a late-night snack at a nearby Irish pub. When he'd walked out of the pub, torrential rain greeted him. The weather had been so bad it had forced him to pull over on the highway because visibility was so poor. Heavy winds as well as thunder and lightning entered the party while he'd waited for visibility to improve enough to continue. Once home, he'd managed to pull into his garage and close the garage door before the power went out.

Power outages in town weren't uncommon, especially in the winter when snowstorms hit. Both Sean and Mack had recommended he invest in a generator for such occasions.

Although it was on his wish list, he hadn't gotten around to having the house wired for one yet. Right now he was kicking himself for that, because no power meant no coffee unless he drove over to Peggy Sue's. Even worse, it meant no running water because, like many of the homes in town, his house used well water, and no power meant the pump on the well didn't work.

Thanks to the emergency release, Dakota got his car out of the garage. Once in the driveway, he got a better look at the damage the storm had caused. Tree limbs and leaves covered his yard as well as his neighbors' yards. One particularly large limb had come off the maple near the side of his house. Thankfully, instead of going through the window, it was leaning against it. Later, it and the other limbs and branches would need to be taken care of.

Unlike the tree near his house, which had only lost a few limbs and some branches, the maple in front of Mack's house had come down completely. It was a good thing Mack's neighbor was never there, because the tree was now blocking the driveway, making it impossible for anyone to drive in or out. On his way home, he'd stop and see if Mack wanted help getting rid of the thing.

Judging by the full parking lot and the line of customers inside, everyone in town had headed to Peggy Sue's this morning for something hot to drink before they tackled the mess left behind by the storm. Despite the extra customers, the employees kept the line moving quickly, and Dakota didn't wait much longer than usual for his extra-large coffee and a cinnamon roll.

With every table and booth occupied, he headed back toward the entrance. He could drink his coffee and eat as easily in his car as he could in here.

"Dakota."

Hearing his name, he stopped and glanced around. He

only knew a handful of women in town, and the voice didn't register. His eyes landed on the table near the front window. Immediately, Mia waved at him. No, correction. It wasn't Sean's wife calling to him. It was his sister-in-law, Angie.

She's Mia's sister, he reminded himself as he crossed to her table. Unfortunately, the reminder didn't switch off the nerves that had suddenly kicked on. As an FBI agent, he'd spoken with everyone from CEOs of major corporations and world-renowned researchers to drug dealers. None of them made him nervous in the least. He hated that the prospect of talking to Angie could.

"Morning. How are you?"

"Better now that I've had some caffeine." Angie held up her paper coffee cup and gave it a little shake. "If you need a place to sit, you're welcome to join me." She gestured toward the empty chair at the table.

Sorry, Mack. Seeing if you need help will have to wait a few minutes. "Power out at your house too?" He settled into the chair and pulled the cover off his cup so the coffee could cool a bit.

"Yep. I think the whole town might be out. I saw a lot of power lines down on my drive over. A lot of trees are down too. One landed on the shed in my backyard. I was going to replace it anyway, but now I need to get rid of it and the tree."

"I'm not sure how, but a limb just missed going through one of my windows. It was certainly quite the storm last night. I had to pull over on my way home from Boston because the visibility was so bad."

"Mia said the same thing when she called earlier to make sure everything was okay. I slept through the whole thing. I didn't even hear the tree in the back come down. Unfortunately, according to Mia, it kept Natalie up most of the night."

Dakota sipped the extra-sweet and creamy liquid in his

cup. "I'm not surprised it kept her up. Kept me up too."
Setting the cup down again, he reached into the paper bag and
pulled out the cinnamon roll.

"Once I'm asleep, it takes a lot to wake me."

"Wish I had that problem. Even the sound of the house
settling at night sometimes wakes me up. Last winter there
were mice in my attic, and I had to sleep with earplugs until
the pest control company took care of the problem." It was
amazing how much noise the tiny creatures made.

Angie cringed when he mentioned mice. Both his mom
and sister were petrified of them. Spiders and snakes, no
matter their size, didn't bother them, but mice sent them
screaming. He'd deal with a mouse rather than a snake
any day.

"Not a fan?"

"In nature they're fine. I just don't want them in
my house."

He'd lived in more than one old house and knew firsthand
it wasn't uncommon for the furry creatures to find their way
inside them, especially in the winter. If she didn't know that,
he wasn't going to be the one to tell her.

Angie folded up the napkin in front of her and added it to
the tray. "Sean recommended I have a company come out and
seal up any openings mice or squirrels might use to get
inside. I set something up for next week. Hopefully, I don't
get any unwanted roommates between now and then."

"I'll keep my fingers crossed for you. Other than that, are
you all moved in?"

She shook her head. "Not even close, but a few things
were delivered yesterday. I didn't want to get too much and
have it be in the way while the renovations are being done.
But it turns out I didn't order enough. Mia and I are going
shopping today."

"How are the renovations going?"

Before she could answer, the cell phone near her coffee chimed, and she picked it up to check the message. "Shoot." She typed back a message before putting the cover back on her coffee cup. "I didn't realize it was so late. That was Mia wanting to know where I am. I was supposed to be at her house ten minutes ago." She reached for the tray containing the remnants of her breakfast order.

"Don't worry about it. I'll take care of it before I go."

"Thank you." She started to push back her chair but then stopped. "I don't know what your schedule looks like, but do you want to meet for coffee or dinner this week?"

He'd had women ask him out before today. Usually they were women he worked with or saw at the gym. Regardless, they were all individuals who lived in the same world as him.

Angelina Troy was in a category all her own.

Dakota wasn't going to let it stop him from saying yes.

"Sure." He mentally ran through his upcoming week. While every week tended to be busy, this one looked to be busier than normal. "Does either Wednesday or Friday night work for you?" Unless something unexpected popped up, those were the most likely nights for getting out of the office on time this week.

His response earned him a dazzling smile, and two dimples he'd never seen in any pictures of her showed up. He didn't know if they were usually removed from photos before they were printed or what, but they made her appear less like an unapproachable actress and more like the pretty girl next door.

"Let's plan on Wednesday." Angie pulled a pen out of her purse and jotted her phone number on a napkin. "Call me later and we can figure out a time."

"Will do."

He watched her walk out. Before he slipped the napkin inside his wallet, he added her number to his cell phone's contact list, because Angelina Troy's number wasn't one he wanted to lose.

When he pulled up to the curb in front of Mack's, his friend and a guy Dakota didn't know were exiting the house.

"How's it going, Mack?" he called out, coming around the front of his car.

"Hey." Mack headed in his direction, and his companion followed. "Dakota, this is Sean's friend Brett. He got into town last night."

Since Mack's neighbor was rarely around, Sean checked on the house regularly and had since the man bought it. Other than to say the owner was in the military and a mutual friend of his sister, Charlie, Sean never shared any details about the individual. And until today Mack had never met him either.

"Welcome to town." Dakota held out his hand. "I live a few houses down."

Brett shook his hand. "Thanks."

Crossing his arms over his chest, he nodded toward the tree blocking part of Brett's driveway. "Looks like Jessie got her wish." Since at least the fall, Jessie had wanted Mack to get rid of the tree growing in the front yard so she could replace it with a flower garden instead.

"She was definitely happy when she looked out and saw it down. Grace already pulled out the gardening magazines so they can get ideas of what to plant there. I tried to tell her Jessie won't be planting anything for a long time, but she insisted."

Considering the size of Jessie at the moment, Dakota didn't think she could bend to tie her shoes, never mind to plant some flowers.

"Did you have any damage at your house?" Mack asked.

Dakota shook his head. "Just a few limbs came down. Nothing serious. Lost power though."

"Told you to get a generator." Mack gestured toward the house. "There's coffee inside if you want some."

"Grabbed some before I came over." And he was damn glad he had. If he'd stopped here earlier instead of going to Peggy Sue's, he wouldn't now have plans with Angie.

THREE

ALTHOUGH THE TOWN once again had power, some residents were still cleaning up after the crazy weekend storm. In fact, several were dealing with much worse than downed limbs and scattered leaves. At the house they just passed, a local contractor was replacing two of the downstairs windows, destroyed when a large limb went through them.

The sound of a chainsaw ripped through the otherwise-quiet afternoon as Angie and Mia approached the stop sign, another clear reminder she was no longer in Southern California.

"Any luck convincing Mom to stay at the Victorian Rose when she comes?"

Mia adjusted the canopy on Natalie's stroller to block out more of the sun. With it being such a gorgeous morning, they'd decided to head out for a walk before the humidity made it impossible. "Not yet."

She'd rather not have Mom stay with her either, but if it would help make the visit less painful for her sister and brother-in-law, she'd offer. "I can ask her to stay with me."

"Your house isn't exactly ready for visitors. Where would

she sleep? On the sofa? On an air mattress? We both know she'd never go for that."

True enough, but the situation could be easily rectified before their parents' arrival. "I can get one of the upstairs rooms ready for her and Dad." She'd planned to hold off on filling any of the rooms with too much, but if the remodelers didn't start on the room until after Mom's visit, any furniture could be moved or put into storage.

"Are you sure?"

"Positive. I know how she gets around Sean."

"Thank you. I really appreciate it. I know Sean will too."

Turning the corner, they headed down Lincoln Street. When they approached a house under construction, Mia stopped. "Looks like Kelsey's house is coming along." She pointed toward the home where several construction trucks were parked in the driveway. "It burned down earlier this year. Some kind of electrical issue. She lost everything."

Angie ran through the names of the people she'd met in North Salem "Kelsey" didn't jump out at her. "Have I met her?"

"I'm not sure. She was at the wedding. Kelsey, Ella, and Cat are close friends. She sometimes joins the monthly poker games. And before I forget again, we're hosting the game in September if you want to come."

"Count me in. Maybe you can give me a crash course on how to play sometime between now and then."

Mia waved to a woman outside another home as they continued down the street. "I can try, but Sean's better at it. Dakota always does well too."

"We haven't even gone out yet." But, man, she was really looking forward to Wednesday night. "It might turn out to be a onetime thing."

"I'm thinking positive. What's wrong with hoping you

fall madly in love with a nice guy and decide to stay in North Salem permanently?"

Her sister the optimist. Some things never changed. "Nothing, but be careful what you wish for. I might decide to stay and then end up at your house every day, raiding your fridge and driving you and Sean crazy."

Since they were on the topic of her making North Salem her permanent residence, now was as good a time as any to ask Mia some personal questions. "Do you ever regret your decision to give up acting and move here?"

Her sister didn't hesitate to answer. "Nope. Even before I met Sean, I felt like I needed a change. I just didn't know what kind until I came here and met him. Honestly, I can't imagine going back to my old life. Mom insists I'll wake up one day and realize what a mistake I made, and then it'll be too late. Sometimes Avery does too. But they're both wrong."

Angie knew Mom's opinion well. She'd shared it enough times with her when the subject of Mia and Sean came up during conversations. Avery, on the other hand, never said anything derogatory about Sean, but she did share Mom's opinion regarding Mia's decision to stop acting.

"On Saturday, you were talking about more than just making North Salem your permanent home when you said you didn't know if you were going back to California."

She nodded. "Avery thinks I'm nuts, but yeah. I started looking at some graduate programs in the area, and I've started writing again."

She'd been twelve when she wrote her first story. She'd continued to write until her sophomore year of college, when she'd made the mistake of showing a completed manuscript to her mom. While Mom hadn't come right out and said it was terrible, she encouraged her to give up writing and instead pursue an acting career like her sister after graduation.

"Good. You never should've stopped. You're a fantastic writer."

Her biggest fan, Mia had read almost everything she'd written and had always loved it—or at least claimed to love it.

"What schools have you checked out so far?"

When it came to colleges and universities, there was no shortage of them in the area.

"Harvard, Boston University, and Northeastern."

The employee standing near the dark purple and yellow Door2Door Express delivery truck parked at a house up ahead waved as they approached. Rather than simply return the gesture and continue on, Mia stopped.

"Hi, Shane. How are you?"

Although not possible, it seemed like her sister knew everyone in town.

"Not bad. I haven't seen you in Masterson's in weeks. Is everything okay?"

"We're still not taking Natalie out much."

Did the man work at Masterson's? Was that why he looked familiar to her?

"Shane, this is my sister Angie. She bought a house in town."

The man's full attention turned Angie's way. "Nice to meet you. I'm sure I'll see you around." He pulled down the back door of the truck. "Enjoy your walk."

They waited until the delivery truck backed out of the driveway before continuing down the street. "He looks familiar," Angie commented.

"Shane works part-time at Masterson's as a waiter. I don't know how he manages it all. According to Mrs. Mitchell, he's enrolled at Salem State too."

Now Mrs. Mitchell she'd met, and from the little Mia had

shared, not a single thing occurred in town that she didn't know about. "Is there anything she doesn't know?"

Mia laughed and reached for the water bottle in the stroller's beverage holder. "Probably not. I bet she even already knows you're in town."

SHE'S FINALLY BACK. Before turning the corner, Shane checked his rearview mirror long enough to get another glimpse of Angie and Mia. The memory of the first time they met played through his mind as he drove to his next delivery.

The weekend after St. Patrick's Day, she'd come into Masterson's with Mia and Sean for dinner and they were seated at one of his tables. She'd smiled at him, and it'd been like a bolt of lightning struck him. He'd fallen in love with her right then. And she'd fallen for him too. Although she'd left town a few days later, he'd known she'd be back for him. But after a couple of months passed and he still heard nothing, he'd started to wonder if maybe he'd imagined the connection that night. When he'd overheard that she'd made an offer on a house in town, he'd known it was Angie's way of telling him she was coming back to him without drawing attention to their love. If the media found out, they'd be all over it. She wanted to keep their love a secret. It'd been hard, but he'd kept the truth to himself, even though what he really wanted to do was tell the entire world Angelina Troy belonged to him.

But now she was back in town and they could proceed with their life together. They wouldn't be able to do it in North Salem. Residents here liked to stick their noses into everyone's business. They always had. It was why Mom moved the family to Danvers when he was a high school freshman.

Tonight when he got home, he'd start looking for a house for them. Maybe something up in the White Mountains. It was one of his favorite places to go. And up there they wouldn't have to worry about the media or anyone else bothering them. Nope, it would be just the two of them. Exactly the way it should be.

FOUR

UNEXPECTED CHANGES and situations were part of the job. Most days he rolled with whatever came his way. Occasionally those unexpected situations left Dakota wishing he still worked for the computer company he'd gotten his first position with after college. Wednesday had been one of those days. He'd been about to power off his computer when a last-minute break in one of his cases came in and forced him to cancel his plans with Angie so he could follow up on the lead. Although it provided him with excellent information, he would've preferred it had come in a day or two later.

When he'd called Angie to break the news, he'd been prepared for any type of reaction. In the past, when work forced him to reschedule plans with a woman, he'd received a range of different responses, some of which were less than understanding.

Angie had been cool about it. Rather than complain or tell him to forget about their date altogether, both things a few women had done to him, she'd wished him luck and asked if Friday night would work for him.

Barring an emergency, work was behind him until

Monday, and tonight he had an evening out with a woman he definitely wanted to get to know better.

Since yellow tape hung across the bottom of the driveway, telling visitors not to drive on the newly paved area, Dakota parked at the curb behind the white convertible in front of Angie's house. Before exiting his car, he grabbed the flowers he'd picked up on his way home from the city. Back in high school when he started dating, one of the first things his dad did was sit him down and give him two pieces of advice, the first being to always treat a woman the way you'd want a man who was dating your sister to treat her. Dad's second suggestion had been to bring flowers on the first date no matter who asked whom out. The talk may have happened close to twenty years ago, but Dakota still followed both suggestions.

A dirt path stretched from the new driveway across the lawn and to the front steps. A pallet of stone pavers sat nearby, waiting to be installed. Well-manicured shrubs of various sizes and flowers occupied the space under the windows. For a moment, Dakota paused in the middle of the yard so he could get a better look at the place. The brick structure was by far the largest house on the street, and judging by the design of the other homes around, it was also the oldest. Despite its age, the place looked as though it had been well cared for over the countless decades. He was glad. All too often, historic structures such as this were left to slowly deteriorate until they were uninhabitable or knocked down to make room for new construction.

Getting his feet to move the rest of the way across the lawn took more effort than it should have. He went after drug dealers and gang members and never flinched. Yet at the moment, sweat that had nothing to do with the outside temperature trickled down his back, and forget about his stomach. It felt worse than the day he'd stood up in front of his entire senior class and given a speech about why they should elect him as their class president.

Pull it together and ring the damn bell. His nerves didn't listen to the command, but his hand did.

Despite the smile, Angie appeared slightly agitated when she opened the door. "Please come in. I'm more or less ready to go. I just need to end a conference call."

"Take your time." He held out the bouquet before he entered. "These are for you."

"They're beautiful. Thank you. And no matter what else my sister or agent has to say, neither of them is going to change my mind. So I promise this won't take long." She took a step back so he could enter. "Make yourself at home. Other than the kitchen, only that room has any furniture at the moment." She pointed to the first doorway on his right. "Be right back. Promise."

Closing the door, he watched her walk down the hall toward the rear of the house. Although not dressed as casually as the day he'd seen her at Peggy Sue's, her outfit and makeup were much more subdued than when she appeared on magazine covers and on the internet. He couldn't speak for other men, but he much preferred her as she appeared tonight. In general he didn't care for a lot of makeup on women. And while he appreciated the sight of a beautiful woman in a bikini as much as the next guy, he didn't understand some women's need to go out dressed in as little clothing as possible all the time.

Left alone for the moment, he wandered into the room she'd indicated.

Since his move to town, he'd wondered about the inside of this house. A lover of architecture regardless of the period, he'd traveled through much of New England since his reloca-tion to the area and toured numerous historical homes and buildings. No matter the style of the home, two of his favorite features in them were the fireplaces and the mantels built around them. Whoever designed the fireplace and mantel in this room had known what they were doing. The same could be said of the built-in bookcases and the molding around the windows.

At the moment, the space between the two candle sconces was empty, but the slight discoloration of the wall over the fireplace showed evidence that a picture or maybe a mirror had hung there for a long time. Other than that minor blemish, it looked like the room had been well cared for over the years and in his opinion didn't need a single renovation. If the other rooms were anything like this one, Angie was wasting her money by having renovations done.

"Sorry about that."

Angie's statement pulled his attention away from the woodwork and toward the doorway.

"Neither my agent nor my sister—who is also my assistant—wanted to accept no as my answer tonight." She joined him near the bookcases. "Even when I told them I had company, they wouldn't give it a rest."

"Don't worry about it. It gave me a chance to check out the woodwork in here."

She ran a hand over the mantel and nodded. "This is one of my favorite rooms in the house. But the detailing in the other rooms is great too. If you think we have time, I can show you."

Dakota checked his watch. Assuming they hit every light just right, they'd have time for a quick tour before dinner. He'd rather not chance it and end up losing their table. "We'd be cutting it close. But I'd love to get a look around. How about when I bring you home?"

"Sure."

He knew Angie had visited North Salem countless times to see her sister, but he wasn't sure how far out of town she'd ventured. To help her expand her knowledge of the area, he made them dinner reservations at a restaurant in downtown Salem rather than at a place in town. Getting them away from town would also allow them time to get to know each other better without igniting the North Salem gossip line—something that was easy to do.

The Liberty Tavern on Hardy Street was located in what had once been a wealthy sea captain's home in the nineteenth century. Although best known for its seafood and steak, the restaurant had a diverse menu, which was exactly why he'd selected it rather than his favorite Italian restaurant a few blocks over.

Window boxes overflowing with colorful flowers adorned the first-level windows at the front of the converted home. With a mix of flowering plants and shrubs flanking the front entrance, the establishment resembled a private residence or a bed-and-breakfast more than an upscale restaurant.

"I need whoever does the gardening here to come and take care of it at my house." Dakota held open the door and then followed Angie inside.

"Yeah, I don't have much of a green thumb either. But the previous owners left me the name of the landscapers they used for years. I've already contacted them about taking care of regular maintenance."

"At least you have something for them to work with. Other than a few trees, my yard is devoid of plant life. When the bank foreclosed on the house, the people who owned it tore out every shrub on the property."

It wasn't all they did either, but those damages he hadn't learned about until after he bought the place. While he could understand the anger the previous family must have felt when the bank foreclosed, the damage they'd caused before moving out had been unnecessary. Local teens had added to the interior problems by using the home as their private party location for the two years it remained empty.

A few couples and small groups sat in the waiting area. Not a single person looked up as they walked passed them to the old-fashioned secretary desk where a twentysomething man stood.

"Good evening. Welcome to the Liberty Tavern. Do you have a reservation this evening?" Even as he spoke, the man kept his eyes focused on Angie.

The restaurant's website stated reservations were not required but strongly recommended. He'd stopped in before without a reservation and ended up waiting an hour for a table.

Dakota nodded. "It should be under D. Smith." With a last name as common as Smith, it was always better to give a first initial too.

The man glanced down at the reservation log before looking up again, but his eyes still never quite met Dakota's face. Considering who was standing next to him, Dakota didn't blame the man. He waited for the employee to ask Angie for an autograph or tell her how much he loved her movies. He'd seen it happen to Mia a few times when he'd gone out with her, Sean, and a few of their other friends. Each time it happened, Mia always obliged the fan with a friendly smile and a brief conversation. He guessed Angie would do something similar.

Tonight the request never came. Instead the employee selected two menus from the desk. "Yes. You requested a table on the deck. Please follow me."

Although not large, the second-floor deck allowed four lucky parties to eat lunch or dinner while enjoying the view of the harbor. This evening there wasn't an empty table out there.

Once they were both seated, the employee handed them

each a menu. "Joelle will be your server this evening. She'll be right over." He shot another glance in Angie's direction, and again Dakota waited for him to either request an autograph or at least ask if she was Angelina Troy. But he didn't. Instead he turned and walked away.

"I wasn't sure what types of food you prefer. The restaurant is known for its steak and seafood, but I've never been disappointed with anything I've ordered."

Angie opened the menu on the table in front of her. "I'm not a big fan of spicy hot foods, but otherwise I'm not too fussy."

Well that was one thing they didn't have in common. When it came to food, there was no such thing as too spicy hot.

Neither of them had a chance to decide on a meal before Joelle appeared at their table, set down two glasses of water, and proceeded to list the chef's specials for the night. Much like the host who'd greeted them downstairs, the woman's eyes stayed focused on Angie even when answering his questions. He found it rude, but he couldn't fault her either.

"Take all the time you need," she replied when Dakota explained they needed a few more minutes to decide on entrees.

Rather than leave and get the drinks and appetizer they requested, she took a step closer to the table and leaned forward. "You must get this all the time, but you look just like Angelina Troy, the actress. You're not her, are you? Because I'm a huge fan. I love all her movies, but I think my favorite is *Deceptive Desire*." She'd lowered her voice so much he didn't think anyone else on the deck heard her.

Shaking her head, Angie frowned. "Sorry, no. But a lot of people have told me I look like her. Maybe we're long-lost relations or something."

Joelle accepted the lie without question and straightened

back up. "They say everyone has a twin out there. You must be hers. Anyway, I will be right back with your drinks."

ANGIE HAD NOTICED the way the host kept looking at her when he showed them upstairs and had held her breath, hoping he didn't ask for an autograph or something. When he hadn't said anything, she relaxed and thought maybe they'd make it through dinner without a comment from anyone.

Then the waitress came along and asked the same question as the woman at the airport. Unlike the representative at the car rental place, the waitress didn't have Angie's driver's license and credit card in her hand with the name Angelina Troy clearly printed for anyone to read. She'd made a split-second decision to avoid a potentially excited outburst that would draw attention their way and lied. Something she rarely did.

Now she was second-guessing her decision. Dakota knew she'd lied. How would that affect his opinion of her? In general, no one liked or trusted liars. She certainly didn't.

Unfortunately, she wouldn't know if she kept staring at the view instead of Dakota. Turning her gaze away from the harbor, Angie expected to see an expression of annoyance or maybe disdain on his face.

Instead she found herself on the receiving end of the same killer smile he'd given her when she opened the door. And much like earlier, it warmed her from head to toe and left her momentarily speechless.

"You know, now that she mentioned it, I do see a resemblance between you and Angelina Troy. I don't know how I missed it before." His eyes danced with laughter. Reaching out, he picked up his water glass. "If she ever needs a looka-like to play her twin in a movie, she should contact you."

If he could joke about it, she might as well play along too.

"Or if she needs a stunt double for a role. I hear they get paid rather well."

"Does she do action movies? I've never heard her name attached to any." He sipped his water, but his eyes never left hers.

She shrugged. "Beats me. I'm not a fan of her movies."

Joelle appeared with their wine, putting a halt to their ridiculous conversation. "Your appetizer should be out shortly. If you need anything in the meantime, please just let me know."

Dakota waited until the waitress left before speaking again. "There is a comedy club a few streets over. I've been a few times. I thought we could stop in after dinner, unless you had something else in mind."

He knew the restaurants in the area much better than she did, so although she'd invited him out tonight, she'd asked him to arrange their plans for dinner. But she had done a search for possible things to do at night in the city when he shared they had reservations at a restaurant in Salem.

She might not have a Grammy-award-winning voice, but she loved to sing, even if it was only in the shower. In fact, one of her favorite presents from Santa had been the karaoke machine she found under the tree when she was ten. "I was going to suggest we go to The Half Door. Now I'm not sure karaoke is the best idea for tonight."

If she were alone, she wouldn't care if people came up and asked for an autograph and a picture or went on about how much they loved her movies. Even if she were with a fellow actor or a musician, she wouldn't mind. They, like her, were used to the attention. Dakota wasn't. While he knew exactly who she was, she didn't want fans reminding him of the fact all night long. Not only that, she didn't want to spend the next couple of hours lying to people, like she'd done with the waitress, either.

"I'll leave it up to you. Either is fine with me. Last time I attempted karaoke was in college on a dare. But I've been to The Half Door with friends. They serve some unique beers. The place has decent food too."

A dare? That sounded interesting. Maybe later she'd have to ask him about it. "Let's try the comedy club tonight."

"Sounds good."

Plans settled on, Angie moved their conversation toward more personal areas. She knew Dakota wasn't originally from Massachusetts, that he worked for the FBI, and had a smile that made her want to get to know him better. Other than those three things, she knew very little about the man. And it just wouldn't do.

FIVE

"MY GOD, he was hilarious. My sides hurt from laughing so hard. I'll never hear any of those songs again and not think of him." The comedian had done an entire show about misheard song lyrics, and she'd laughed from the start of his routine until the very end.

Dakota's arm brushed against hers as they walked toward the public parking lot. "Last time I saw him, he did a similar act but with different songs. I think it might have been better than the one tonight."

"He must sit and listen to music all day." Angie moved closer to the storefronts so the large group heading toward them could pass by, and Dakota followed.

"Our last stop of the evening before returning to the visitor center will be The Burying Point Cemetery. It is the second-oldest cemetery in the United States as well as the final resting place of John Hathorne, one of the local magistrates involved with the Salem Witch Trials," a man dressed all in black wearing a stovepipe-style top hat explained to the men and women following him as the group walked by them and continued down the sidewalk.

"Is that one of those ghost tours?" She pointed over her shoulder.

Entering the parking lot, he glanced back at the group stopped at the next intersection. "Most likely. They're popular around here. I've seen advertisements for some in Boston too."

"Mia told me about one she went on a few years ago. She loved it. Do they run every night, or are they only on the weekends?"

He opened the car door and waited for her to get inside. "I don't know about the ones here, but in Boston they have them every night until around early November. It's probably the same here."

A late-night ghost tour sounded like a great second date, assuming Dakota was interested. She might be wrong, but she got the impression he would be. Throughout dinner he'd been attentive and willing to discuss any topic she brought up. Perhaps best of all, not once did he monopolize the conversation, which was a truly refreshing change from some of the more recent dates she'd been on. Really, there was nothing worse than being with someone who didn't let you get a single word into the conversation.

While she watched him walk around the front of the car, she pulled her cell phone from her purse. She'd heard it chirp twice, indicating she'd received some new text messages during dinner, but had ignored it. If she'd received any more texts while in the comedy club, she hadn't heard the device over the continuous laughter filling the place.

Avery's name was attached to both of the messages she'd received during dinner as well as one that had come in sometime after they left the restaurant. Her personal assistant or not, her older sister could wait until tomorrow for a reply.

She slipped the device back into her purse as Dakota got behind the wheel.

"Are you interested in stopping somewhere for dessert?" He started the car and cranked up the air conditioning.

The Liberty Restaurant had an excellent dessert menu. Unfortunately, they'd both been too full to order anything off it after dinner.

"Maureen dropped off a welcome basket yesterday with all kinds of goodies, including a homemade blueberry pie and cookies. If I don't share it with someone, I'm going to eat everything in it myself."

"You had me the second you said Maureen. That woman can bake."

No sooner had she unlocked the front door than the sound of her cell phone chirping came from her purse.

Not now.

Ignoring the device, she switched on some lights and dropped the purse near the stairs. She'd promised him a tour of the house and planned on giving him one with no interruptions from Avery or anyone else. "Which would you prefer first, the tour or dessert?"

"Since Maureen did the baking, let's have dessert first."

She'd made the first move by asking him out. Keeping with that trend, she reached out and took his hand. "If you want, I can make some coffee or tea."

"Whatever you're having."

Another chirp came from her purse before they made it halfway down the hall.

"Do you want to check that first?"

She'd ignored Avery's texts, and if her sister hated anything, it was being ignored. Most likely these new messages were more from her. "Not really." But if it wasn't Avery and instead Mia, it could be important. "But I probably should."

Releasing his hand, she backtracked to where she'd left her purse and checked the device. Sure enough, the newest texts were more from her eldest sister. Rather than ignore them as well, she typed back a quick reply letting Avery know she'd call sometime tomorrow morning.

"Everything okay?" This time she didn't have to reach for his hand. Dakota took hers when she moved close again.

"It's just my sister wanting to pick up where we left off earlier. I think Avery forgot about the time difference between us."

"If it's important, I don't mind if you call her back."

She appreciated the gesture but had no plans to take him up on it. "Regardless of whether I call her now or tomorrow, she'll get the same answer. And she's not going to like it any more than she did earlier tonight."

HE WALKED in the room and had to do a double take. While the little he'd seen of the house remained period specific, the kitchen resembled something out of a 1980s TV sitcom, right down to the yellow countertop and linoleum-covered floor.

"I'm not sure what the previous owners were thinking when they decorated this room. I hate it. It's my least favorite room in the house."

Dakota understood why too. If he owned the place, the kitchen would be first on his list of areas to renovate.

"At least you have cabinets on the walls. I didn't have any when I moved in. The previous owners pulled them all out before they left."

Angie opened the door on the mustard-yellow refrigerator and reached in for the blueberry pie on the top shelf. "Sounds like a bitchy thing to do." She set the dessert down on the table before filling a teakettle with water. "If the interior designer I hired ever gets things right, this will be one of the first rooms they tackle. Right after the master bathroom, because I need a shower."

She might not agree with it, but he saw no harm in sharing his opinion. "I haven't seen the rest of the house, but so far only this room needs an overhaul."

He watched her move from the stove to the cabinets on the opposite wall. Each stride was fluid and graceful, reminding him of countless ballerinas he'd watched when his older sister had danced with the Phoenix Ballet Company.

"I agree, and that's the problem. Except for in this room and the master bath, I don't want to destroy what's already here. But the designer's vision for the place includes removing the built-in bookcases and covering up the fire-places. We're meeting again next week." Cutting into the pie, she handed him a large slice before cutting a second, much smaller one. "Hopefully I'll like what he comes up with next. I'd like things done or at least almost done before my mom comes in October. She's staying with me instead of Mia and Sean."

Dakota imagined the change in plans thrilled his friend. "How long is she staying?"

"Too long."

He couldn't help but laugh. She sounded about as pleased to have her mom coming as Sean had the other night. "Diffi-cult person to live with?"

"You could say that. Between you and me, I'd rather have her stay somewhere else. But at least if she's here with me, it'll be better for Mia and Sean. If it was my dad, he could move in with me and I wouldn't mind."

Both his parents had been strict, and he'd been anxious to live on his own, but he had an excellent relationship with them. It didn't sound like that was the case between Angie and her mom.

"Is your dad coming too?" Sean hadn't mentioned whether his father-in-law was visiting or not, and he hadn't asked. When it came to his friend's in-laws, it was better not to bring them up.

"Yes, but not for long. He's not a big fan of being away from home or work, so he'll only be here a week. Mom plans to stay for two." An emotion bordering on dread filled her voice. "But she might decide to stay longer. She did when she visited right after Natalie was born. According to Mia, things got pretty tense between Mom and Sean, and he considered staying at the Victorian Rose until she left."

He remembered the visit back in June. Sean had spent some extra time at Dakota's house helping him finish the upstairs master bathroom even though Dakota could've handled it himself.

Leaving the table, Angie removed the whistling teapot from the stove and poured the boiling water into two mugs. "Do you want milk or sugar for your tea?"

"Black is good."

She handed him a mug before adding a generous splash of milk to her tea. "Do your parents visit a lot?"

"No. I usually fly out to Arizona instead. Mom will fly but hates doing it. I've never seen anyone more nervous on a plane than her. My brother usually flies home to visit for the same reason, and my sister only lives a couple of hours away from my parents."

"Are they older or younger?"

"Both older."

Angie folded her hands on the table and leaned forward. "Let me guess, they never let you forget it either."

Truer words had never been spoken. "Bill used to remind me every chance he got. Anne was better, but she sometimes acted as if she was my mother."

"Sounds like they'd both get along well with Avery." She smiled, and the two dimples he'd noticed days ago appeared.

Other than at Sean and Mia's wedding, he'd never seen

Avery. As far as he knew, she hadn't visited town since the wedding.

"Avery's three years older than Mia and five years older than me. And she never used to let us forget it."

After a second slice of pie and several cookies, they remained sitting at the kitchen table sharing more details about their families.

"Your mom gave you each a name that started with the letter A so you'd all have the same initials as her?" He didn't get confused easily, but he felt like he was missing a piece of a puzzle right now. "Isn't your mom's name Lynn?" When he wasn't calling her a less-than-complimentary name, Sean called his mother-in-law Lynn.

Finishing her tea, Angie set the mug back down. "It's what everyone calls her, but her name is really Agatha. She hates it and has always gone by her middle name."

Well, the name *was* a little old-fashioned, and it wouldn't be a name he'd pick for a daughter if he ever had one. "And Lynn is her middle name."

"Yep. And for some crazy reason, she wanted all her children to have the same initials as her. I'm Angelina Lori, Mia's full name is Amelia Linette, and Avery's middle name is Lydia."

He wouldn't call it crazy, but naming your children so they had the same initials as you was unique. "My mom teaches English literature, and she named my brother and sister after characters from two of her favorite books. She even spelled my sister's name with an *e* at the end because it was how the character in *Anne of Green Gables* insisted on spelling it."

"And what book did she use to name your brother?"

"*Pride and Prejudice.*" A book he'd never read, but he had suffered through two different movie versions.

"I've never read it, but I saw the movie. I don't remember a character named Bill or even William."

She wasn't wrong. "Technically the character's name is Fitzwilliam. According to my brother's birth certificate, his name is Fitzwilliam. But he's always gone by either William or Bill." He'd never blamed his brother either. Fitzwilliam wasn't a name you heard every day anymore, and he wouldn't want it.

"She didn't name you after a favorite character?"

He'd gotten the same question from others when they learned his siblings were named after characters from novels. "She planned to. They thought they were having a girl, and Mom decided on Scarlet."

"*Gone With The Wind* fan?"

"Big time." His mom read the book every summer. He'd tried it once to humor her but didn't get past the first few chapters. "Mom and Dad weren't expecting me for another month, so my parents took my brother and sister camping. They were in South Dakota visiting Mount Rushmore when Mom went into labor." He'd heard the story so many times it was like he'd experienced it. "When it turned out I was a boy and not the girl they were expecting, they needed to come up with a new name. Mom suggested Dakota as a way to remember the trip."

"I guess it's a good thing they weren't camping in Rhode Island or Oregon when your mom went into labor."

"True, but Texas or Montana might have been okay."

She drummed her fingertips against the table. Unlike his fingers, they were long and slender with well-manicured fingernails. "Tex Smith does have a nice ring to it."

The same hand he'd held over an hour ago reached for her plate. Unlike his, it contained half of her second slice of pie. "I really want to try the fudge, but I can't eat anything else." She carried both the plate and her mug to the counter.

Collecting his plate and empty mug, he brought them over to her. "If you'd mentioned the fudge earlier, I would've skipped the cookies."

"I didn't mention it earlier so you'd have to come back over if you want to try it."

"Really?"

She feigned an innocent expression and shrugged. "What can I say? I like to plan ahead."

They might not have the same taste in food, but in that regard they were similar. He'd started running through possibilities for other evenings out the moment they left the comedy club. "Does that mean you have plans for tomorrow night?"

"Depends. Are you free?"

He didn't feel any urgent need to go on one, but when the group walked by, she'd seemed interested in the ghost tour. "I thought I'd go on a ghost tour in Salem. When I get home, I can make the reservation for two instead of one if you're interested."

"I'll bring the fudge along with us so we have something to snack on." She added the pie plates to the ancient dishwasher and stepped closer to him. "Is it too late, or do you still want a tour of the house?" Reaching out, she slipped her fingertips down his forearm, leaving a trail of excited nerve endings behind before reaching for his hand.

Too late? He felt more awake now than when he'd climbed out of bed this morning. "It's not even close to my bedtime."

In her heels they were the same height, and if he took a single step closer, he'd be able to kiss her. At that moment, he wanted to kiss her more than he wanted to take another breath. He forced his feet and his lips to stay exactly where they were though.

Her feet seemed to have other ideas. With a single step,

she eliminated whatever space existed between them and her body brushed against his.

Releasing his hands, she put her arms over his shoulders and moved her face closer to his. "Good."

Angie's lips came down on his before his brain finished giving his lips the okay to kiss her. And then for the next few seconds, his brain didn't think at all.

If he'd had the heart rate monitor he wore when he ran, it would've been in the red zone by the time she ended their kiss.

"I've wanted to do that since I opened the door," she admitted.

One thing he could say about Angie, she wasn't shy about making the first move. He didn't know many women like that, and he found it sexy as hell.

Angie took a step away from him. "I don't want to keep you up past your bedtime. Let's get the tour in."

She kept her hand wrapped around his as she led him from one room to the next on the first floor and then up the front staircase. Although holding hands was an innocent gesture, one he'd experienced countless times before, tonight it was doing some crazy things to his insides. Things he hadn't experienced in a damn long time.

"I saved this one for last."

Bigger than the first two rooms she'd showed him upstairs, this one remained empty as well. And like in its counterparts, a large fireplace took up a decent amount of one wall. However, unlike the other two, this one contained narrow built-in bookcases on either side of it. Although a nice room, he saw no reason she'd want to save it for last.

"At first, I thought these were built-in bookcases like the ones downstairs in the library." Angie moved them closer to the fireplace. "But only that one is." She pointed to the one on the left side of the fireplace before releasing his hand.

With a tug, she pulled the other one open like a door, revealing the space and ladder behind it. "The ladder leads up to a small room in the attic."

He'd toured houses before with secret hidden rooms, although in some cases calling them rooms was misleading. Some were more like crawl spaces. Regardless of size, people had used them for everything from hiding runaway slaves prior to the Civil War to hiding liquor during Prohibition.

"Any idea what it was used for?"

"No, the only thing I found up there was some old Christmas wrapping paper, so at least someone who lived here hid their presents up there. Mia thinks there might be some information about the house at the town's historical society. I need to make an appointment to visit."

"Talk about a great place to stash presents from your kids so they don't find them."

"Or hide. I wouldn't want to spend a lot of time up there, especially since it doesn't have any windows, but if a person needed to hide, it'd be a great spot."

Angie closed the door, and once again it appeared as though two simple bookcases flanked the fireplace. Unless someone knew the truth, no one would ever think to try to move either of them.

Except for the room with the closed door, the one that must be Angie's bedroom since none of the other rooms up here contained any furniture, she'd taken him through all the rooms on the second floor. As much as he hated to admit it, that meant their evening together had come to an end.

"Do you want me to make the reservations for tomorrow, or do you want to handle it?" Earlier he'd offered, but he wanted to make sure she was still okay with it. Several companies offered ghost tours. Although they were probably all similar, one might appeal more to Angie than another, and since she was the one who wanted to go, she might want to choose.

She considered his comment before answering. "I'll take care of it. Mia really enjoyed the one she went on, so I'll check with her in the morning and ask her which one it was. After I make the reservations, I'll call you."

"Sounds like a plan." In the kitchen, she'd kissed him. Now, he took the initiative. He brushed his thumb across her jaw before touching his lips to hers.

Although intended to be a simple goodnight kiss, it sent his stomach into a tailspin and erased almost all intelligent thought from his head. Somehow he managed to grab on to the last thread of it, and he pulled back.

"See you tomorrow."

Angie moved several steps back before finally releasing his left hand. "Looking forward to it."

SIX

SHANE NEVER CALLED IN SICK. Even when he'd had the flu over the winter, he'd gone to work and attended classes. Yesterday, for the first time since being hired by Door2Door Express, he'd done just that, because the sooner he found them a place, the sooner they could start their life together.

He'd emailed the real estate agent a list of the places he wanted to see, and she'd also found a few she thought might interest him. They'd met at her office in Conway and spent the morning visiting both homes for sale as well as locations for rent. While some had potential, only one had been exactly what he wanted. And unfortunately that one was just out of his price range. Although the agent admitted he could make a lower offer, she doubted the owners would accept anything other than the asking price, especially since she was bringing in two other parties to look at it this weekend alone.

After looking at each location and making a quick stop back at the real estate agent's office, he'd checked into one of the local chain motels in the area, frustrated but not defeated. He'd just started the search. Sure, he'd hoped to find the ideal house this weekend and make an offer, but he wasn't stupid.

Sometimes it took a few tries before you found the right one. It'd even taken him two weeks to find his current apartment when he'd first moved out of his mother's house, and he hadn't been all that particular then. Since this would be the house where he and Angie spent the rest of their lives and raised their children, it had to be perfect. Perfect didn't happen overnight; it took time and patience. And patience was something he'd always had an abundance of.

Today, as much as he'd rather check out some more properties, he returned to North Salem. Door2Door Express provided him with paid sick leave, but Masterson's did not. If he missed his shift at the restaurant, his income this month would be lower, which meant less money into his savings account for their new house.

Several children were at the playground on the town common as he passed by. He'd never spent much time there as a kid. Mom refused to let him go by himself, and she'd never seemed to have the time to take him over. Forget about his father. He'd spent as much time away from town as possible even before the divorce. After the divorce, he moved out of North Salem and never showed his face again. When he and Angie had kids, he'd make sure they had their own private playground in the backyard. Their children's playground would have not only swings and a slide but also a climbing wall and a fireman's pole. Maybe he'd build them a tree house too.

Parking in the lot behind his apartment building, he closed his eyes. Off in the distance, he saw the top of Mount Washington, and a few feet ahead of him stood a swing set complete with two slides and a fireman's pole. A pregnant Angie stood pushing a young girl with long dark hair on a swing. With each push, the little girl laughed and urged Angie to push her higher.

Whack. The happy family image disappeared, and Shane's

eyes opened to find Chandler, his neighbor from across the hall, knocking on the car window. The same age, they'd attended elementary and middle school together. Back then they hadn't hung out. Since his move back to town, they'd developed a friendly relationship and would occasionally grab a beer together or watch a ball game.

Grabbing his cell phone and keys, Shane stepped out of the car. "Hey, what's up?"

"Not much. Heading into work." A part-time sales representative for a medical supply company, Chandler worked as a personal trainer on the weekends at a nearby gym. "I stopped by last night to see if you wanted to watch the game, but you weren't around."

Friend or not, he wasn't going to share with Chandler his plans to buy a house and move. "Went to my mom's for dinner. She'd been after me for weeks to visit. Finally gave in to shut her up."

"You missed a hell of a game. If you're interested, I'm meeting Gary and Jon at O'Leary's for some pool around six. Join us."

They'd still be there long after his shift at the restaurant ended, but he had more important things to do tonight. "I'll keep it in mind."

ANGIE LINGERED at her place long enough to bathe and enjoy a morning coffee before driving over to her sister's house. While she could've gotten the name of the ghost tour company over the phone, a call wouldn't let her visit with her niece. It'd only been a few days since she last saw Natalie, but she already missed her. Angie really didn't understand how Mom, Dad, and Avery managed to stay away. In all fairness, Avery hadn't met Mia and Sean's daughter yet. Maybe if her older sister took the time to visit, she'd fall in love with their niece as well and think twice about living so far away.

Max was busy sunbathing in the front yard when she pulled into the driveway, but he popped right up and met her before she closed the car door. "Hey. I don't blame you for soaking up some rays today."

The sky was crystal clear, making it an ideal day for sunbathing, an activity she might engage in today depending on how long she visited with Mia. Angie gave the dog a scratch behind the ears, and like an obedient usher, he walked alongside her to the front door.

Although her sister was expecting her, Sean answered the door, not Mia. He had Natalie against his shoulder, his large hands supporting her head and tiny body. For perhaps the thousandth time, she mentally shook her head. While he might not be someone who could further Mia's career, Sean was a great guy who loved her sister and adored their daughter. Instead of accepting him and Mia's decision to leave acting, Mom constantly told her sister what a mistake she'd made and tried to convince her to divorce Sean and salvage her career before it was too late.

Sean gave her a one-armed hug and then closed the door. "Mia went up to take a quick shower. Natalie decided her breakfast belonged in her mom's hair instead of in her stomach."

She touched the baby's little fist. "I can't believe someone so sweet would do something so mean."

Kissing the top of his daughter's head, he started walking toward the living room. "Believe it. This wasn't first the time Natalie's eaten and decided the meal would look better on one of us." Rather than settle Natalie in one of the many baby-safe contraptions in the room, he sat and repositioned her against his chest. "Mia told me Lynn is staying with you when she comes. Thank you."

"Not a problem."

The look Sean sent her said he knew she was lying but wasn't going to say anything. "Any progress with the interior designer?"

Angie made herself comfortable in an armchair across from Sean. "We're getting closer. I have my fingers crossed that when I meet with him this week, I can give his plans the green light. When I want to relax, I love a long hot bath, but I need a shower in the house."

"Taking the time to fill a bathtub every morning would drive me nuts. If you meet with the guy and still don't like his plans, I can remodel the master bathroom for you."

She'd seen the gorgeous master bathroom he'd completed upstairs, so he was certainly capable of remodeling hers, but a project like that would take considerable time. Time he'd rather spend with his family, and they both knew it. "I'll keep it in mind."

They sat chatting about nothing specific until Mia joined them. Her sister looked tired but otherwise happy as she plopped down on the sofa next to her husband. Carefully, Sean transferred Natalie to Mia before kissing her on the cheek.

"I'll be back in a few hours," he said, coming to his feet. "Do you need anything while I'm out?"

Mia started to shake her head but then paused. "Actually, if you think of it, can you grab some bread? We're almost out."

"Will do." Sean kissed Mia again and then Natalie before looking Angie's way. "Remember what I said about your bathroom. I don't mind."

"I will, promise."

With Sean gone, Mia turned her full attention Angie's way. "I know you've already dismissed his offer, but Sean really loves remodeling. I think he's bored now that he finished all the projects around here. And I think they've just about finished everything at Dakota's house too."

Last night Dakota had mentioned the previous owners of his house had torn out all the cabinets in the kitchen before moving out. Other than the kitchen, she wondered what other rooms the owners had damaged.

"And speaking of Dakota, how was your date last night?"

The image of them kissing near the front door flashed through her mind, and a ripple of anticipation passed through her. The kiss had been tender and as light as a summer breeze, but it had left her mouth burning and wanting more. "Good."

Mia's shoulders slumped, and she frowned. "Just good? I was hoping you two would hit it off."

"We're going out again tonight." Angie's comment earned her a glare.

"If you're going out again, it must have been more than just good."

She couldn't help but laugh. "You're right. I just wanted to see what your reaction would be."

Angie would admit giving Mia a hard time might not be nice, but sometimes it was simply fun. And if the tables were reversed and Mia had gone out with one of Angie's friends, her sister would consider doing the same thing. Of course, neither would ever think about doing it to Avery. She didn't have much of a sense of humor and took herself way too seriously.

"I had a great time. We had dinner at the Liberty Tavern and then went to a comedy club in Salem. Afterward we filled up on some of the treats in the basket Maureen brought me."

"And?"

"And I gave him a tour of the house. He seemed really interested in the architecture."

Her sister rolled her eyes. "The man has a mouth that screams 'kiss me.' So did you?"

She didn't disagree, but once again she couldn't resist the opportunity to give Mia a hard time. "You've noticed?"

"Believe me, I've noticed. I'm married, not dead. Dakota's smile is one in a million. If you had a nice enough time to go on a second date, you must have kissed. So how was it?"

"As fabulous as you'd expect." Since her sister hadn't offered, Angie gestured toward her niece. "Can I hold her?"

Mia didn't hesitate to stand and bring Natalie over. "Sure. It's been over an hour since she ate, so it should be safe. I don't know about you, but I haven't eaten yet. Do you want something to drink or eat?"

Her stomach rumbled, reminding her she hadn't eaten today either. "How about both?"

"Follow me."

She'd been in the kitchen more times than she could count, but she hadn't really paid much attention to its features. While her sister set out what looked like homemade blueberry bread and plates, she took in the details. Often in homes similar to this one, the kitchen was a place to prepare food but not linger. Angie hadn't seen the original kitchen, but she assumed this one had been no different. That was no longer case. Now the room was not only a place to cook meals but also where the family could sit down and enjoy them. It was exactly the type of kitchen she wanted in her house.

"Before I leave, I want to take a few pictures of this room so I can email them to Gregg. Maybe then he'll have a better idea of what I'm looking for." She wished she'd thought of doing that a week ago. If she had, maybe they would've made more headway by now.

Mia placed two cups of tea down. "Take pictures of whatever you want." She got the milk from the refrigerator and added it to the table, then sat. "What are you and Dakota doing tonight?"

"A ghost tour in Salem. Do you remember the name of the one you and Sean went on?" She transferred Natalie to her left arm so she could eat. "Since you enjoyed it so much, I thought I'd make reservations with them."

"I've got to think about it. I remember the tour started at the Hamilton Hotel. And Sean and I had dinner at The Scarlet Letter, the restaurant in the hotel, before the tour." Mia's forehead pinched with concentration as she poured milk into her tea.

Angie was about to suggest they just do a search for ghost tours that started at the hotel when Mia snapped her fingers.

"Bewitched Footsteps. When you go, make sure you wear comfortable shoes. It's a long tour with a lot of walking. I made the mistake of wearing heels, and we couldn't finish."

Before she forgot the name, she brought up the website and made reservations. Then she sent Dakota a text message letting him know what time she'd pick him up. She didn't get a chance to slip the device back in her pocket before a text from Avery popped up. Even though she'd known her sister would reach out again today, she sighed.

"What's wrong? Are they booked tonight?"

Eyeing the message, she considered her response. "I made reservations." She pointed to the cell phone. "Avery sent me another text. She sent me several last night too, and that was after a lengthy conference call with her and Skylar. I promised to call her back today, but evidently she couldn't wait."

"Let me guess, they found the perfect project for you." Before Avery worked as her personal assistant, she'd been Mia's. The same was true of Angie's agent, Skylar Henderson. Both women were disappointed when Mia decided to focus on her family and finishing the degree she'd started years ago rather than her acting career.

"Yep. And I'm not interested, but they don't want to hear it. Especially Avery." Although both women worked for her, Skylar respected the employee/employer relationship far better than Avery, who considered herself an older sister first and a personal assistant second. Angie typed a short message promising to call as soon as she got home. Then she put the device on vibrate so her sister could send as many more texts as she wanted and Angie wouldn't have to hear the phone chirp a thousand times.

"Then you've decided to stick around here for a while."

The vision of Dakota handing her flowers and bestowing one of his killer smiles took center stage in her thoughts. "That's my plan."

SWEAT SLID down Dakota's back, making his T-shirt stick to his skin. He enjoyed exercising, but he hated running. If it were up to him, swimming instead of running would be part of his weekly workout program. But like a lot of things in life, it wasn't up to him. Every year the Bureau required all agents to take a physical fitness test, and running, not swimming, was part of it. So at least three days a week, he ran. During the nice weather, he did it outside, because if he had to do it, he might as well be able to enjoy some fresh air. When it rained or was simply too cold, he used the treadmill at the gym.

For a change of scenery, he'd tried a new route today and run from his house to the bike trail that started down near the Stonefield Dam and continued into Marblehead. When he'd started out, he had the trail mostly to himself, but as he headed back into town and the park, more and more people passed by him. He could see the two granite posts marking the end of the trail when his cell phone dinged, interrupting the song coming through his earbuds. Slowing his pace, he pulled the device out of the armband strapped around his bicep.

Dakota, we have reservations for tonight. Tour starts at 8:30. Okay if I pick you up around 8:00?

He anticipated doing the driving again tonight, but she could take care of it if she wanted.

If you want to come by around 6:30, I'll grill us dinner.

He didn't bake breads or cookies, and the meals he made on the stove didn't always turn out the way he intended, but he was a master with the grill.

Various meal ideas floated through his mind as he walked off the bike trail and started for the street.

What can I bring?

He didn't have to think before answering her question.

Just you.

If you think of anything else, let me know.

Dakota crossed Lincoln Street and broke into a slow jog again. The sooner he got home and cleaned up, the sooner he could drive over to the butcher in Danvers. The meat selection at the grocery store in town was adequate, but it didn't compare to the one at the butcher. Meat wasn't the only thing they sold either. They usually had a good selection of fresh vegetables from nearby farms as well as a decent selection of wine. While over there, he'd stop at the bakery next door and grab something for dessert. The same family who owned the butcher operated it, but he'd never gone in before. Since it was right next door, it would allow him to make one less stop today.

Before heading up to the shower, Dakota made a quick detour to the large deck off the kitchen. One of the few features of the house the previous owners hadn't destroyed, it stood only a foot or so off the ground and stretched from the back of the house around to the left-hand side. Near the center of the deck, three steps led down to the stone walkway that encircled the in-ground pool, another feature that had remained untouched while the house was empty. Closer to the house, a hot tub large enough for perhaps four adults was set into the deck. Regardless of the temperature outside, he enjoyed soaking in the hot tub, especially on those more stressful days at work.

After checking to make sure the grill had gas, he turned to head back inside. His eyes fell on the hot tub. If Angie brought along a swimsuit, they could come back after the tour and enjoy a soak. Of course, if she preferred going in naked, something he did occasionally, he wouldn't complain either.

Pulling his phone out, he typed out a message suggesting she bring a bathing suit. Rather than send the text, he deleted it. This was only their second evening together. If he sent the message he'd just deleted, she might interpret it to mean he expected more than her company tonight. And he didn't. Well, unless fudge counted as expecting more than an enjoyable evening out. Last night she had promised to bring along what Maureen added to the welcome basket. Fudge, homemade or store bought, wasn't something he'd ever turn down.

He glanced around one last time. A few leaves and some pollen covered the patio tables and chairs, but he'd have more than enough time to clean both when he got back. Entering the kitchen, he left his cell phone on the counter and headed upstairs, somehow more eager for the evening ahead than he'd been last night—a fact he'd thought impossible.

SEVEN

THE WHINE of the siren from either an ambulance or fire truck suddenly filled the air. It was a sound Dakota heard on a regular basis, because both the fire station and the police station were within walking distance of his house. To stay informed of what went on around town, he checked the monthly report log both stations published, so he knew that usually when the ambulance went out, it was for nonlife-threatening injuries. It was a similar situation for the fire trucks. While they did have the occasional severe house fire, most of the time when they went on a call, it was for either small structural fires or car accidents. He sincerely hoped whatever the call was now it was a minor one.

A second siren disturbed the silence again as he opened the front door. The sound barely registered thanks to the vision standing on his steps. Unlike last night, Angie was dressed much more casually today in khaki-colored shorts that showed off just how long her legs really were. She'd paired them with a light purple tank top that, although snug, didn't look like it might cut off all the circulation in her upper body. It did, however, accentuate her breasts, and he knew for the next several hours he'd have to remind himself not to stare. She'd pulled her long dark hair into a ponytail, giving her that girl-next-door look. She'd also kept her makeup light.

Last night he'd kissed her as a way to say goodbye, so he saw no reason not to kiss her now as a way to say hello. Unlike last night, he didn't let his lips linger on hers, although they certainly wanted to.

"I hope you're hungry," he said after they exchanged a verbal greeting.

Her eyes drifted to the vicinity of his mouth for a brief moment and then met his as her lips spread in a smile—one that had him thinking about what he was really hungry for, and it definitely wasn't the filets on the grill.

"Starving." She held up a plastic container. "Almost ate all this on my way over." Angie pulled off the cover, revealing a box full of chocolate squares.

Filets might be on the grill, but he couldn't resist the sugary treat on display and plucked one from the container. "I almost sent you a text reminding you to bring this today." The dense chocolate fudge laced with peanut butter melted in his mouth. "Wow. That. Is. Good." He eyed the container, contemplating a second piece. Rather than reaching inside, he took Angie's hand and helped her put the cover back on. "Do whatever you have to, but don't let me eat any more until after dinner."

One of her dark eyebrows arched. "Whatever I have to?"

Desire and excitement ripped through him, and his feet moved him closer before his brain realized what his body was doing. Lowering his face toward hers, he stopped just before their lips touched.

"Whatever." He whispered the word against her mouth before covering it with his. This time he took his time, learning the shape and feel of her lips before coaxing them apart so he could learn the taste of her too.

Angie's free hand settled on his neck as her breasts pressed into his chest. The intimate contact sent an instant message to the blood in his body, and it all rushed south of his belt buckle. With her so close, he doubted there was any way she wouldn't notice. But at the moment there wasn't a damn thing he could do about it.

He allowed himself one last pass over her lips before he pulled back. It was either end the kiss or recommend they continue their greeting while naked and in the hot tub. Since he didn't want to pressure her into doing anything, ending the kiss seemed the better of the two ideas.

"I have everything set up for us to eat outside." After locking the front door, he took her hand and led her through the living room and into the kitchen.

Leaving the fudge on the counter, she glanced around the room. "Did you do all the work in here?"

The kitchen had been the first project he'd tackled after buying the home. Although a professional might have done a slightly better job, he liked the way the room turned out. "For the most part, but a few friends helped me out. Especially Sean. The guy's an expert when it comes to remodeling houses."

"Is this the only room you remodeled?"

After taking a bottle of red wine from the small wine fridge he'd incorporated when he renovated the kitchen, he removed the cork. "No. When I moved in, every room needed something done. On their way out, the previous owners took their frustrations out everywhere. Then while it sat empty, local high school kids made it their private party house. I guess that's what I get for buying a foreclosed property. Live and learn."

He handed her a glass of red wine and gestured toward the glass doors. "Unless you prefer your meat well done, the filets are just about ready."

"Medium rare is perfect for me. Avery likes hers well done, and I don't know how she eats it. She even likes her chicken and pork overcooked to the point you can barely get a knife through it."

She took a sip from her glass and followed him outside. Although they weren't touching, energy buzzed through his body. He wanted nothing more than to pull her close again and taste the wine on her lips.

"I'd say this makes up for the lack of shrubs in the front." Angie gestured around the deck and yard. "I'd trade all the flowers and plants in my yard for a pool and hot tub any day. I didn't realize how much I'd miss both until I didn't have either. Both are on my list of things to have installed."

Dakota opened the grill cover, and after checking the internal temperature of both filets, he removed them. "You're free to use either whenever you want. I had a heater installed on the pool in June, so I'll keep it open until about the end of September."

"If I had a bathing suit with me, I'd take you up on the offer now."

Don't let the lack of a bathing suit stop you. He added the filets to the other dishes on the table before readjusting the umbrella so the sun didn't roast them both alive. Then before he suggested they skip dinner and go for a late afternoon swim naked, he moved their conversation on to a new topic.

"Did you take care of whatever Avery wanted to talk to you about last night?"

In his opinion, talk of family was often a good way to keep desire in check. It also gave him the opportunity to learn more about her besides what the media printed or Sean told him. Last night they'd made a good start at getting to know each other, but a single date could only accomplish so much.

Angie added a little of everything to her plate before opening her napkin and placing it on her lap. "I called her after I got home from Mia's. It wasn't a pleasant conversation. She'll probably call again in a few days and try to change my mind. When it comes to things like this, Avery is rather predictable. Stubborn too. She takes after my mom."

It wasn't any of his business, but he was too curious not to ask, especially since she'd said something similar last night. "Change your mind about what?"

"Viking Studios plans to make a sequel to *A Prince to Call Her Own.* They want me to resume the role I played in the movie. I already told my agent and Avery I'm not interested in doing the sequel. Skylar's accepted my decision, or at least I think she has. Avery and my mom are another story."

Angie sliced into her meat and popped a piece in her mouth. She took two more bites before continuing. "They both want me to spend a few weeks here visiting with Mia and Natalie and then get back to what they call my 'real life.'" She made air quotes as she said the words and rolled her eyes. "For the hundredth time, I told Avery that I'm changing my real life. Not long after our chat, Mom and I had a video call so she could pick up where my sister left off. Thanks to modern technology, I was able to witness the eruption of Mount Vesuvius firsthand."

Not for the first time, he was glad Lynn Troy wasn't his mother. Mom shared her opinion freely even if you didn't ask her for it, but she'd always accepted the decisions he and his siblings made. "That bad?"

She nodded, and the end of her long ponytail slipped over her shoulder, cascading over her chest. Dakota's fingers itched to move the hair back over her shoulder and replace it with his hand.

"It doesn't matter. I'm not changing my mind. Next week I'm going to get my driver's license changed and register to vote. I want to vote in the upcoming special election this December."

"Then your house here isn't just so you have a place to stay when you visit Mia and Sean?"

"Nope. My move here is permanent. I love California, but I miss the East Coast, and Mia and Sean aren't the only family members I have living in Massachusetts. My grandparents still live here, as well as my aunts, uncles, and most of my cousins. And since I can write from anywhere, I'm going to stay here so I can be close to all of them."

She'd left him with a great opportunity to learn more about her without bringing up topics she didn't want to discuss tonight. "What do you write?"

OTHER THAN MIA, she never discussed her writing or her desire to become an author and screenwriter with anyone, and that included her mom and eldest sister. But not only did Dakota seem genuinely interested, she wanted to tell him about it and allow him to get to know her rather than the Angelina Troy the media sold to fans. Unfortunately, once she got going on the topic, it got away from her and she ended up monopolizing much of their conversation over a delicious dinner. If Dakota minded, though, he didn't let on.

"Yours or a rental?" he asked as they approached the driveway.

"Rental. Until I figure out what I want, I'll keep this." She loved convertibles. At the moment, she had three different ones in her garage in California, but North Salem got snow in the winter. An SUV with all-wheel drive might be a better option for day-to-day driving.

"If I were you, I'd consider something a little more substantial than this one. At least for during the winter."

"I was thinking the same thing." She used the key fob to unlock the doors and walked around to the driver side. "The tour starts at the Hamilton Hotel. Do you know where it is, or should I put the address in the GPS?"

"It's not too far from where we were last night." He waited until she was behind the wheel before speaking again. "Did you book us the same tour your sister went on?"

"Yep. She warned me it's a long one, so I took her advice and wore sneakers." He probably couldn't see them, but she pointed at the dark purple canvas sneakers on her feet.

Located on the corner of Washington Square and Derby Street, the Hamilton Hotel was an excellent example of the luxury hotels built in the early twentieth century.

Dakota opened the glass door before she could touch the handle. "I've driven by this hotel, but I've never been inside. I heard they used it in a couple of horror movies back in the 70s. Supposedly it's haunted."

Since the tour started here, that made sense. After all, why would you start a tour in a building that wasn't rumored to be haunted when Salem had so many locations that were?

He let the door go and reached for her hand. "Do you know where we're supposed to meet the group?"

"The website said downstairs in the library." Before leaving for Dakota's house, she'd spent about thirty minutes reading over the tour company's website. Besides listing the various locations visited and giving some details about each of them, it gave some history about the city itself.

With its low ceiling, wood-paneled walls, and nautical decorations, the library resembled a sea captain's quarters on an old ship, or at least how they appeared in films. Lights shaped like old-fashioned lanterns hung on the walls, and a dark blue carpet covered the floor. Several comfy-looking chairs and a few tables occupied the room, making it an ideal spot for hotel guests to retreat and read a book or work. At the moment the room was empty except for the woman seated near a door marked Staff Only. When she spotted Dakota and Angie, she stood up.

In a dark dress with long flowing sleeves, the woman wore her long, dark gray hair loose down her back. "Are you here for this evening's tour?"

"Yes, I made reservations this afternoon." Angie pulled up the confirmation number on her cell phone.

The tour guide moved closer and slipped on the eyeglasses hanging around her neck. "Welcome. You're a little early, but that's fine. We have ten other people joining us tonight." After checking the number against a list on her clipboard, she looked up at them and then down at her list again. "You're not by any chance the Angelina Troy who stared in *A Prince to Call Her Own*? If you're not, you look just like her."

She could give the woman the same line she'd given the waitress last night. But unlike last night, the guide had not just their confirmation number on her list but also their names. Rather than lie, something she still felt guilty about doing yesterday, she nodded. "I recently moved to the area."

The guide's eyes tripled in size. "I can't believe you're going on one of my tours. I love your movies. A few weeks ago, I read they're making a sequel to *A Prince to Call Her Own*. Will you be in it? The article said Chad DeMelo already signed on, but it didn't mention you or Anderson Brady."

Since she was being honest, she got ready to tell the guide she wouldn't be in the sequel. But the woman didn't pause long enough for Angie to speak.

"If you don't, the movie won't be the same without the

two of you. The chemistry between you and Anderson jumped off the screen. And when the love scene near the end between you and Anderson came on, I thought I was going to go up in smoke. If you and Chad had done the scene I probably would've. Don't get me wrong, Anderson is a cutie, but Chad's my man."

Chad might have a slight edge on Anderson in the looks department, but his personality canceled it out. His fans might not know it, but Chad was a first-class ass. Anderson, on the other hand, was one of the nicest guys in the world.

The woman checked her watch. "Would you mind taking a picture with me before the rest of the group arrives?"

Honestly, she'd prefer not to, but unless impossible when a fan requested, she always obliged. "Sure." Angie glanced at Dakota, who'd not made a sound or moved from his spot next to her. "Do you mind taking it for us?"

"Nope." He accepted the cell phone the guide retrieved.

Dakota snapped a few pictures before handing the device back. The guide slipped the phone back into the small backpack on the floor before more voices let them know additional guests were on their way down.

Not wanting to be the first person the other members of the group saw, Angie grabbed Dakota's hand and dragged him toward the back of the library where the lighting was dim.

"Love scene, huh?" he whispered in her ear. "It doesn't sound like my usual type of movie, but I might have to check out *A Prince to Call Her Own*."

"She's exaggerating. It wasn't very steamy."

The look Dakota sent her suggested he wasn't buying it.

Near the front of the room, the guide welcomed the other members of the group to the tour. Not once did the woman glance their way or let on that Angie was any different from the other people booked for the evening's tour. She hoped it stayed that way. Angie didn't want to spend the night posing for pictures with strangers.

Once the guide checked everyone in, she stepped in front of the wall lined with bookshelves. "Again, I want to welcome each of you and thank you all for choosing Bewitched Footsteps. My name is Missy Carr, and this is my tenth season doing tours for the company. If you've been on tours with us before, you'll notice we've added a few new stops and temporarily removed a couple."

The lights in the room dimmed further.

"But as always our tour tonight begins here at the Hamilton Hotel, where the spirit of ten-year-old Lizzie Scranton resides."

Angie remembered seeing the girl's name mentioned on the website, but she hadn't taken the time to read the story attached to it.

"Long before they built the Hamilton Hotel in 1920, a prominent sea captain by the name of Gilbert Scranton built his home on this location. On his last trip across the Atlantic to England, Captain Scranton took his wife, Emma, with him, and they left their daughter, Lizzie, behind with her nanny. On their return trip home, their ship sank during a storm. Everyone on board perished. After the death of her parents, Lizzie bounced between various relatives for three years until she died from pneumonia at the young age of ten."

An extra-cold blast of air blew down on her from the air-conditioning vent in the ceiling. Whether coincidental or planned, the people in front of them started whispering amongst themselves.

"For years residants of the Scranton home caught glimpses of Lizzie running up and down the halls. Even though the owners of the Hamilton tore the home down in 1919 to build the hotel, sightings of Lizzie never stopped. Countless people, including me and my husband, have seen her down here and on the third floor, waiting for her parents to return home."

Angie wasn't sure whether or not she believed in ghosts, but she still glanced around the room like everyone else.

"Our tour this evening will last approximately two hours and will take us all around Salem. If you have any questions, please don't hesitate to ask. If at any point you become too tired to finish, I understand. I can radio back and have a hotel shuttle come pick you up. All you need to do is let me know. Does anyone have any questions before we head out?" Missy looked around the room, but her eyes didn't seem to linger on them longer than the other guests.

A woman near the front raised her hand. "Can we take pictures while inside the buildings?"

"In some of them, yes. Those stops that do not allow photography will have a sign posted. Anyone else?"

When no one else spoke up, Missy waved toward the stairs. "Then everyone please follow me."

The steady hum of multiple conversations followed the group as it obediently filed up the stairs and across the lobby behind Missy.

"What a sad story," Angie whispered from their spot at the back of the group. She didn't always get along with her mom, but she couldn't imagine growing up without her.

"Even now sailing across the ocean can be dangerous, and we have all kinds of technology. I think we forget how much more dangerous it was over a hundred years ago," Dakota replied.

Compared to the frigid temperature inside the library, the warm summer air was perfect. Before she could make the first move, Dakota slipped his arm around her waist, his hand settling on her hip. Despite the fabric between them, the heat from his hand burned through her shorts and caused her thoughts to travel away from the tour and to how hot his hand would feel against her bare skin.

In front of them, the group came to a sudden stop. Behind Missy stood an old cemetery.

"This is the first of three cemeteries we will visit tonight. The second will be The Burying Point Cemetery. It dates back to 1637 and is one of the oldest in the country. The final one will be the Howard Street Cemetery. Although that one wasn't established until 1801, the location where the cemetery now stands is supposedly where Giles Corey was pressed to death in 1692."

Missy pointed to the area behind her. "This cemetery dates to 1779. Over the years people have seen many spirits wandering between the headstones and sitting on the bench under the maple tree. The most frequent sightings are of a young man and woman dressed in Civil War-era clothing. Local residents have long believed they are the spirits of Fitzgerald Wilson and Anne Montgomery."

Desiring more physical contact, Angie looped her arm around Dakota's waist and tried to focus more on Missy's story and less on what Dakota would look like sans clothing. It wasn't an easy task.

"The couple fell in love despite the fact that Anne came from a wealthy, prominent Salem family while Fitzgerald worked as a footman in a nearby mansion. Not long after the Civil War broke out, Fitzgerald joined the Union Army. He died during the battle of Gettysburg in July 1863. When Anne learned of his death weeks later, she committed suicide. Anne's parents buried her here in the Montgomery family plot. Fitzgerald's grave is unknown. The first sightings of Anne and Fitzgerald began a year after her death and have continued ever since. In fact, I saw them earlier this summer for the first time." Missy gestured toward the open gate.

"Please feel free to look around. We will exit through the gate at the far end of the cemetery."

"Talk about another sad story." Dakota kept his voice low so no one else would overhear.

She expected to hear several more before the night ended. "I think a lot of hauntings are attached to sad or devastating events."

They passed by the weathered headstones. Some she could read, but others appeared as nothing more than blank slabs, and unlike cemeteries still in use, there were no flowers or flags decorating each burial site. Regardless, the cemetery was well maintained.

Once everyone was through the gate at the other end, Missy turned right. "Our second stop this evening will be the Turner-Ingersoll Mansion. Thanks to author Nathaniel Hawthorne, today most people know the house as The House of Seven Gables."

Angie included. Until this moment she'd assumed the home had always been called The House of Seven Gables. "Did you know it's called the Turner-Ingersoll Mansion?"

"Yeah, but only because I took a tour of the house about a year ago so I could check out the architecture." Dakota's warm breath teased her ear as he whispered, and she wished his breath was teasing other parts of her body.

She'd gotten the impression he was interested in architecture last night. It sounded like she'd been right.

Using today's standards, few people would call the structure in front of them a mansion. Compared to the houses that would've been around it at the time, though, Angie understood how it earned the label.

"I know you're all anxious to go inside, but first I'd like to give you a little history about the home behind me. Captain John Turner built the house in 1668, and it is the oldest surviving seventeenth-century wooden mansion in New

England. In 1782, Captain Samuel Ingersoll purchased the home. Upon the captain's death, his daughter, Susanna Ingersoll, inherited the property. Many visitors have reported seeing Susanna Ingersoll, Nathaniel Hawthorne's cousin, roaming the halls. There have also been reports of a boy running and playing up in the attic. I have never heard a boy running, but I have seen Susanna numerous times over the years. If we're lucky, perhaps she will make an appearance tonight. Now, unless someone has a question, let's head in."

When no one spoke up, Missy pushed open the door and led everyone inside.

They both remained quiet as they walked through the various rooms. But when they left the building and started for the second cemetery on the tour, Angie held back so the rest of the group could get ahead of them. She wanted to be able to have a conversation and not interfere with anything Missy was sharing.

"You seem into architecture the same way my sister is into history." No one toured old homes to see the architecture unless they had a significant interest in it.

"For a long time, I planned to study it in college." He released her hand and put his arm across her shoulders, bringing her closer as they followed the group down the street.

Excitement and longing surged through her, and she wrapped her arm around his waist. "Why didn't you?"

"My dad was never a big supporter of the idea. He thought I should study something with greater employment opportunities. He constantly told me to keep an open mind about other options. Then my sophomore year of high school, an agent from the FBI came to career day. After listening to her talk, I started to reconsider my plan. I did some research into what the Bureau looks for in applicants. Degrees in architecture were not among the top ones they looked for.

Degrees in computers and engineering were, so I got an undergraduate degree in computer science and then a master's in computer science with a concentration in cybersecurity. Not long after I earned my master's, I applied to the Bureau."

The rest of the group stopped in front of a house, signaling to Angie to put a temporary halt to their private conversation.

"Behind me is the Jonathan Corwin House. Sometimes people refer to it as The Witch House." Missy gestured over her shoulder at the gray home. "Judge Corwin was a local magistrate and civic leader during the time of the Salem witch trials. He investigated the various claims brought against citizens, and he served on the Court of Oyer and Terminer, which sent nineteen citizens to the gallows for witchcraft."

Countless stops and more than an hour later, they were seated in her car and headed back to Dakota's house. Although she hadn't seen anything otherworldly—no one had —it had been a unique way to see the city and learn more about its long history.

"I really enjoyed that. You?"

Dakota took her hand and held it against his thigh. "Actually yeah, I did. It made the history of the area seem more real. I'm glad we went."

The thigh beneath her hand was solid, and she expected it to be as muscular and well sculpted as his arms. The jeans he wore prevented her from finding out for sure. Eventually, she'd hopefully find out what his jeans, as well as the rest of his clothes, were hiding. It just wouldn't be tonight. The media might portray her as being fast and loose, jumping into a guy's bed after spending only a few hours with him.

It was wrong.

She had both male and female friends who acted that way, but she'd never done it. She didn't have to date a guy for months and months before she slept with him, but she needed more than two evenings out. So although images of them together had teased her several times since she walked into his house, she wouldn't be acting any of them out. At least tonight. Depending on how things progressed this week, next weekend was a definite possibility.

EIGHT

SHE SPENT two days researching SUVs as well as other cars. Once she'd settled on the two vehicles she wanted, a Range Rover for the cold snowy months and a new Mercedes convertible for the nice weather, she asked Dakota if he wanted to come shopping with her—for two reasons. First, shopping was always more fun with a partner, and second, although she'd talked to him, Angie hadn't seen him since Saturday night. He'd agreed with no hesitation; however, tonight had been the first night he could guarantee he'd get out of work on time. They'd finished up the shopping part of their evening over a half an hour ago and were now back at his house.

"I've never seen a salesman bend over backward like the one at the dealership tonight. If you'd asked him, I think he would've let you drive the car off the lot tonight without a single penny down. I'm anxious to see if the ones at Gies Auto Mall will be as bad." Dakota set a large bowl of chips down next to the salsa and guacamole already on the coffee table.

Angie didn't tell him such behavior wasn't unusual,

whether she was shopping for jewelry or simply making a reservation at one of her favorite restaurants in New York City. Instead, she kicked off her flip-flops and folded her legs up on the sofa.

"I'm just glad they're going to take care of getting it registered for me. I really didn't want to make another trip to the DMV. Going there to get my new driver's license was enough."

Now that she'd decided on what she wanted, she wanted to get both vehicles purchased and registered so she could cross one more thing off her mental to-do list. Unfortunately, time had been a limiting factor tonight, and they'd only made it to the Mercedes dealer.

Dakota switched on the flat-screen television mounted on the wall but didn't sit down. "Do you want anything else before the game starts?"

When they spoke on Monday, he invited her over to watch the baseball game tonight with him even before she asked him to come along for a little car shopping. She didn't know much about baseball, but she'd accepted anyway.

"All set. Thanks." She had a handsome guy about to sit down next to her, snacks on the table, and a bottle of locally made cola that, according to the label, contained real cane sugar rather than corn syrup, although how it would affect the actual taste, she had no idea.

He didn't waste any time getting comfortable next to her and taking a swig from his bottle of cola.

"Where are they playing tonight?" Other than the names of a few teams and the fact that all the teams wanted to win the World Series at the end of the season, she knew next to nothing about the sport.

"They're in Seattle."

If Boston was playing on the West Coast, it explained why the start time of tonight's game was on the later side.

"They're called the Nationals. Right?" She'd dated a guy who was a Washington Nationals fan.

Dakota looked at her as if a unicorn horn had just sprouted from her head. "Uh, no. The Nationals are from DC, and unless it's during interleague play or the World Series, Boston doesn't face them. The Nationals are in the National League, while Boston is in the American League. The Mariners are from Seattle. You're not into baseball, are you?"

Gee, what gave me away? "It's not that I'm not into it so much as I don't think I've ever seen an actual game."

Now his expression suggested a second unicorn horn had poked its way through her skull. "Never? Not even when you were a kid?"

If she had, she couldn't recall one. "I've seen them in movies and stuff, but Dad's not a baseball fan. He's a huge New England Rebels fan. Watches all their football games on television, and whenever they play on the West Coast, he goes. He's pretty big into hockey too. He played on hockey teams until he graduated from college. And the only sport Mom is into is golf. But she prefers to go golfing, not watch other people play. Not that I blame her." One of her former boyfriends had enjoyed watching golf and had done so every chance he got. Whenever he turned it on, she fell asleep.

A commercial came on the screen, and he muted the volume. "And what about you? Are there any sports you enjoy?"

"Shopping." She snagged a plate and added some chips and salsa to it.

"I'm not sure shopping qualifies as a sport." He followed her lead and added a handful of chips to a plate, then plopped a generous spoonful of guacamole and salsa next to them.

"Trust me, the way Avery and I do it, it does." She lifted a chip covered with salsa toward her mouth. "I enjoy watching the Rebels play, but I've never been the type of person who has to watch football every Sunday. And I enjoy swimming a lot."

Angie bit into the chip and chewed. When he'd brought the snacks in, he mentioned he'd made the salsa yesterday. Even if he hadn't told her, the taste alone would've given away the fact that the stuff in the bowl wasn't from a jar. She dragged another chip through the salsa and popped it in her mouth.

"No sports in high school?" He dipped a chip in first the guacamole and then the salsa.

"Nope. I tried out for the volleyball team my sophomore year but didn't make it. But I was big into school clubs. I was in the drama club all four years of high school, and I worked on the school newspaper one year. In my junior year, I helped form the literary club. Avery is the athletic one. She played a sport during every season." Reaching for her cola, she took a sip. Although the taste resembled the colas produced by the big name companies, this one had a slightly different flavor to it. One she preferred.

"What about Mia? Was she into clubs like you or into sports in school?"

"Neither. After she landed her first role on the series *Family Life*, she never went to school again until college. She always had private tutors, either on the set or at the house. Sometimes I envied her, other times not so much. It's hard to ignore the teacher and daydream when you're working with them one-on-one." They didn't discuss it much, but she knew Mia often regretted not attending school the same way most people did. "Did you play a lot of sports?"

He swallowed the food in his mouth and then licked the salsa off his finger. "I kept busy. Mom wouldn't let me play tackle football. She said it was too dangerous, so I played flag football until I was eleven. In middle school, I started running cross-country in the fall, played basketball in the winter, and baseball in the spring. After I graduated high school, I stopped except for the occasional pickup basketball game."

On the television, the commercial for extra-soft toilet paper ended and the sports announcers for the evening's game appeared on the screen. Picking up the remote, Dakota unmuted the sound but kept the volume low. "Anything you want to know about the game before it starts?"

If he had to take the time to give her a lesson on the rules of baseball, it'd be difficult for him to watch. "Nah, I'm sure I'll figure it out as it goes along." After all, how hard could it be? A person hit the ball and ran some bases.

He increased the volume by a few numbers and placed the remote on the coffee table. "If you have any questions, let me know."

"DO the coaches always argue with the refs like that?"

Should he correct Angie and tell her in baseball they were called umpires, not referees, or let it go? "No, not in every game, but it's not unusual for a coach to disagree with a call made by an umpire and then get into an argument. If the coach goes too far, an umpire can eject him from the game. He can eject players too."

"Then I'm surprised the coach for Boston didn't get thrown out. He was right up in the umpire's face."

Dakota switched off the television and dropped the remote back on the table. Boston had won, and he didn't need to hear the postgame report.

Angling her body in his direction, she tucked one leg up on the sofa. "Why do they call them referees in football, basketball, and soccer but umpires in baseball?"

He'd never wondered about it; it simply was the way it was. "No idea. Maybe someone thought it sounded better?"

Whether they were called referees or umpires, they performed a similar function. "Overall, what did you think of the game?"

To him, it was unfathomable that she'd gone her entire life and never seen a single baseball game. It wasn't like they were talking about Olympic figure skating or something. Baseball was often called America's pastime. A person could probably find a game being shown on either television or streaming on the internet every day of the week once the season started. Some sports channels even played classic baseball games from the 80s and 90s during the off-season.

"Honestly, I think I enjoy watching football a little more. It's faster paced, but I enjoyed the game tonight."

His mom always compared watching a baseball game to watching paint dry and had preferred watching basketball and football. Still, she'd made it to as many of his baseball games as she could.

"I wouldn't mind watching Boston play again."

Since his move to New England, he'd become a die-hard Boston fan, much to the annoyance of his dad, a lifelong New York fan even though he'd never lived in New York or even close to it. Dakota tried to get to a few games every season. This year, he'd only made it to one so far.

"A friend of mine at work has season tickets. Unless they're playing either New York or Tampa Bay, he's always willing to sell a couple. I can talk to him tomorrow and see about getting us some tickets." He could go on the internet and buy tickets for an upcoming game, but he'd never get seats as good as the ones Jimmy had.

"Sounds good."

His eyes followed her every movement as she unfolded her legs and stretched them out. Like the night of the ghost tour, she had on shorts, but unlike the ones she'd worn then, these were much shorter. So short in fact, the edges of the pockets peeped out from below the edge of the denim. When his gaze hit her light purple toenails, he reversed the path and let his eyes trail back up.

Damn, she's got legs. Dakota pictured them entwined with his as they rested after making love. Would they feel as soft as the skin on her hands? They sure as hell looked incredibly smooth.

When she slipped on her flip-flops and stood, the mental picture disappeared and his brain returned to reality.

"I'm going to head out. I know you have work in the morning." She picked up the empty chip bowl and placed the smaller bowls that had held salsa and guacamole inside of it.

Even worse, he had a meeting at eight o'clock tomorrow morning. On a good day with no traffic, he could make the drive from North Salem to Boston in about forty minutes. During the week in the morning, there was always traffic. Some days, especially when it rained or snowed, it took him two hours to reach the office. If he wanted to make sure he arrived at his meeting on time, he'd have to leave the house a little after six. With such an early morning ahead of him, it was best if Angie left now.

What was best and what he wanted were not the same thing tonight.

Dakota collected the empty soda bottles and then took the large bowl from her hands before she made it through the doorway. Angie was a guest in his house. He didn't want her cleaning up for him.

"If I'm running late tomorrow, I'll call and let you know." Since they hadn't made it to both car dealers tonight, they were going to Gies Auto Mall tomorrow night. After depositing everything on the kitchen table, he placed a hand on either side of her waist and pulled her a little closer. "And Boston is playing Seattle again if you want to come back here and watch the game."

He'd left some space between them because his blood was still on fire from the image of her naked legs entwined with his. If his body actually came in contact with hers right now, it might spontaneously combust.

Angie had other ideas and closed the gap between them as her arms snaked over his shoulders. "Sounds good." She lowered her mouth to his.

Her lips were warm and sweet on his, and the tantalizing vision of them naked in his bed reappeared. Moving his hands lower, he slipped them into her back pockets, his palms molding to her ass as if it were created just for his hands.

Exactly how long they stood there, he'd never know, but eventually she pulled back. "I better go."

His first instinct was to tell her she didn't need to go anywhere. But he didn't. He had an early morning, and it was clear she wasn't ready to take this thing between them to the next level. "I'll walk you outside."

North Salem was a safe town and his yard had enough lights, but walking Angie to her car was the proper thing to do. The type of thing he'd want a guy to do for his sister. Of course, walking with her also meant another minute or two with Angie and perhaps another quick goodnight kiss.

The lights on either side of the front door illuminated the steps and front walkway, while the spotlight attached to the garage lit up the driveway. Unlocking the car door, Angie opened it but didn't get inside.

"Thanks for coming with me tonight. See you tomorrow." She dropped a kiss on his lips but didn't linger.

He waited until she backed out of the driveway before returning to the house. Last week when he'd walked into Peggy Sue's because the power was out, he'd expected the visit to the café to lead to nothing but a hot beverage and some food. How wrong he'd been. Where things between them would eventually go was anyone's guess, but he planned to enjoy himself while he found out.

FROM HIS PARKING spot at the curb, Shane kept a watchful eye on the house. Until Monday he hadn't known where Angie's home was. Mrs. Mitchell solved the problem for him though. He'd stopped at the old widow's home to deliver a package. He probably dropped one off at her house at least twice a week. He didn't know what she bought, but she clearly enjoyed shopping online. As often happened, she'd started up a conversation, first telling him how much she was looking forward to her granddaughter coming to live with her. From there she'd gone into how she couldn't believe both Angelina Troy and Brett Sherbrooke, President Warren Sherbrooke's nephew, had moved into town within days of each other. Although he'd heard about both additions, he'd played dumb and asked if she knew where in North Salem they lived. As he'd expected, because this was Mrs. Mitchell and nothing happened in town that she'd didn't know about, she'd known the exact locations of the homes they'd purchased—not that he cared where the hell Brett Sherbrooke lived.

Since then he'd only allowed himself to drive by Angie's house once. Late Monday night after his shift at Masterson's, he'd gone by before heading home. At the time, a white convertible was parked on the street out front, and yellow tape was draped across the end of the newly paved driveway. From the street, he'd seen lights on both downstairs and upstairs. He'd considered hanging around so he might catch a glimpse of Angie as she passed a window, but he'd decided against it.

Tonight, after leaving O'Leary's, where he'd met Chandler and Gary for a few beers and the first half of the baseball game, he headed straight to Grove Street rather than his apartment. He'd been slouched down in his car watching the house ever since. The white convertible he'd previously seen wasn't out front, but the yellow tape across the driveway was no longer there, so the car could be in the garage. However, the entire house remained in darkness, suggesting Angie wasn't home. And if she wasn't, if he sat here long enough, he'd see her when she returned.

Bright headlights appeared farther down the street, and as they got closer, he slouched down more in the front seat. If someone drove by his car and noticed him sitting in it, they would become concerned and most likely call the cops, because people in North Salem were nosy. They always had been and they always would be.

The car didn't keep coming toward him. Instead it turned into Angie's driveway, and he could just make out her profile when the sensor lights on the garage switched on.

She's home. More than anything he wanted to pull into the garage next to her before she closed the door and carry her inside the house. Once inside, he'd bring her up to her bedroom and make love to her. But the time wasn't right. He needed to have their house set and ready first. Then he could take her away from here like she wanted, and they could start their life together.

The garage door closed, and soon after lights appeared in several of the first-floor windows. A few went on upstairs as well. Angie was home safe and sound for the night, which meant it was time for him to head home too.

Shane started the car but kept the headlights switched off. He cast one last look in the direction of her house before shifting the car into Drive. He didn't turn the headlights on until he reached the stop sign at the end of the street.

Soon, Angie. Don't worry, we'll be together soon. I promise, my love.

NINE

ONCE A MONTH STARTING in the spring and ending in August, the town held a block party on the town common. Even before Dakota purchased his house in North Salem, he attended one as a way to appease his curiosity. Since his move into town, he'd attended several more. But each time, he'd gone alone and hung out with the various friends he'd made. Tonight he had other plans.

For the last block party of the season, Angie was accompanying him, and he'd been looking forward to the event ever since he'd invited her Thursday night. Afterward, he hoped she'd come back to his house. She'd done that both on Wednesday and Thursday after they'd gone car shopping. Both nights they'd watched the Boston/Seattle game while getting to know each other better on every level. Although they'd shared some blood-boiling kisses and some intimate caresses, she hadn't given him a clear indication she was ready to be lovers. He couldn't deny he hoped she'd be ready soon. He wasn't sure how many more ice-cold showers his poor skin could handle. On this, though, he was leaving the timing up to her.

He was about to head out to the garage when the cell phone in his pocket chimed. Pulling it out, Dakota found a message from Mack. When he'd passed Mack and Jessie's house on his way home from work last night, he noticed the pink and blue balloons tied to the mailbox outside. Since it had been close to midnight, he waited until late this morning to send Mack his congratulations and ask how everyone was. That had been hours ago.

Thanks. Jessie and the babies are doing great even though they came a little early.

Glad to hear it. Let me know when Jessie will be up for visitors.

Come by anytime. We'll be here until Tuesday.

When his cousin's daughter was born, his wife had only been in the hospital overnight. Maybe it was different when a woman had a C-section. Mack had mentioned one afternoon that it was the plan because one of the babies was in a transverse position. Dakota wasn't entirely sure what that meant, and he hadn't asked for a detailed explanation. As far as he was concerned, some things a guy didn't need to know unless he was about to become a father.

Okay. Maybe tomorrow or Monday after work. I'll call first.

After sending the final message, he headed into the garage.

Thursday night when he picked Angie up, the front walkway had been a work in progress. It was no longer the case. The landscapers she'd hired to take care of the yard had been busy too since his last visit. They had removed the handful of unhealthy-looking shrubs in the yard and replaced them with new ones. While they were at it, they added more colorful flowers, most of which he couldn't identify. Perhaps he should get the name of the landscapers and see what they could do about his yard. It really was a desolate mess out front, and while he cut his own lawn and raked leaves, he'd rather have someone who knew something about shrubs do any planting.

When Angie opened the door, her smile was alive with affection and delight. "Hey, I was about to call to see if you wanted me to meet you at your place instead."

Since they needed to head back toward his house, it would've made more sense for Angie to drive over. Call him a little old-fashioned, but he preferred picking up his dates as opposed to them coming to him. He knew better than to tell Angie or any other woman his sentiments. One never knew what they might deduce from such a statement.

"Don't worry about it. It's not like it was a long drive. I could've walked over if I wanted to."

"True." She moved so he could step inside. Once the door was closed, she put her arms around his neck. "I missed you last night." She whispered the words near his lips before kissing him. "I ended up watching the last game of the series, but it wasn't as much fun alone."

Angie's fingertips traced little circles against the back of his neck. The slight touch cleared any thoughts from his mind and sent a message to the brain behind his zipper telling it to take over. While he'd like nothing better than to listen to that particular body part, he kept his hands locked safely around her waist where they couldn't get into any trouble.

"Believe me, I would've much rather been with you last night." He would've rather sat through his ninth grade French class again than do what he'd been doing last night. On television, conducting surveillance looked exciting. In reality it was, as his mom would say, as much fun as watching paint dry. "I might have to do it again one night this week, depending on what happens this weekend." The office had assigned other agents to cover the downtown café frequented by the suspected mob boss.

"You definitely have a unique job." She kissed him again before moving away, and his body immediately missed the physical contact. "Let me turn off the music and we can go." Angie didn't give him a chance to pull her close before walking away.

The country music coming from the direction of the kitchen switched off, and a moment later she came back down the hallway. She'd pulled on a New England Rebels baseball cap and had a large tote bag over one shoulder and a wristlet dangling between her fingers.

"All ready."

It wasn't any of his business, but if the bag was her new purse, Angie needed to scale back on how much stuff she carried around with her. If she didn't, she risked throwing out her back. "What's in there?" He pointed to the large dark purple bag.

"A bathing suit and a towel. I hoped we could get in a swim or maybe enjoy the hot tub after the block party." She dropped her cell phone and wristlet into the bag.

If she wanted, they could skip the block party altogether and spend the night alone at his house. There would be more parties next season. "We don't have to go over tonight if you'd rather do something else."

Angie shook her head and pulled the front door closed behind them. "If this wasn't the last one until next year, I'd say let's skip it, but I'm too curious to wait until next spring. Mia told me all about these parties, and they sound like nothing I've gone to before."

The monthly block parties were certainly like nothing he'd ever gone to before, and he'd lived in several different places thanks to his father's time in the army. "Then a swim after it is."

A car he didn't recognize was parked in Mack's driveway as they approached the house. A moment later the front door opened, and Socks, the family dog, emerged along with Mack's mom and his daughter Grace. Pulling in behind the car, he put down his window. Right away Grace skipped over, the dog's leash clutched tightly in her hand.

"Hey, Dakota." Grace and her cousin, who was often with her, were two of the friendliest children he'd ever met. Neither seemed to have a shy bone in their body, and whenever he saw either around town, they stopped to say hello. "I have a brother and a sister. Ivy and Ryan were born last night."

Faced with such excitement and happiness, one couldn't help but smile. "Congratulations on becoming a big sister. I'm sure you'll be great at it."

"Dakota, how are you?" Mrs. Ellsbury, Mack's mom, asked, reaching his car.

"Good, you?"

"Wonderful. I became a grandmother for the third time last night. We were just stopping by to collect Socks. Grace will be staying with me until Jessie and Mack come home from the hospital." The older woman's expression matched her granddaughter's as she delivered the news.

"Are you going to the block party?" Grace asked. "Drew will be in the dunk tank tonight. Daddy told me to make sure I dunk him."

He knew the organizers had asked Drew McKenzie, the town's resident sports hero, to go into the dunk tank this weekend. And like Grace, he intended to send his new friend into the water. "We'll be there."

After a few more brief words, Mrs. Ellsbury led Grace and Socks to her car, and Dakota backed out of the driveway.

"Jessie and Mack were at Sean and Mia's wedding, right?" Angie asked.

"Yes. Sean considers Jessie another sister. Charlie and Jessie were best friends growing up. And Mack and Sean were only a couple years apart in school and played sports together." Dakota hit the garage door opener and drove inside.

"And you and Mack work together."

"Correct. Technically he's a Boston cop who works as a task force officer for the FBI. But most of what he does is for the Bureau."

They stopped in his house long enough to drop Angie's bag off before heading back out. If not for the fence surrounding his yard, they could've cut through it to Main Street, the horseshoe-shaped road that went around the town common. Since the eight-foot fence around his yard made doing so impossible, they headed down the street toward the parking lot at St. Mark's Church instead. The lot bordered Main Street, and people attending the block parties often parked there.

He'd come to enough of these by now that the scene before him shouldn't give him pause. Still, it did because in so many ways the party on the common seemed like something taken from a 1960s television show. Residents of all ages moved about the area. Tonight a DJ was set up on the bandstand, cranking out music, but sometimes the town brought in local bands instead. A temporary dance floor covered part of the grass, and people, mostly those in their teens and twenties, moved to the music. Various scents filled the air, and Dakota knew they'd be able to get everything from hamburgers and hot dogs to homemade baked goods if they headed over to the food tables. The dunk tank was near the center of the green, and several feet away from it, inflatable bouncy houses swayed as children jumped inside.

When they reached the edge of the grass, Angie came to a complete standstill. "Wow. This is…. I'm not sure what to call it. Old-fashioned, perhaps. Like something from one of those classic black-and-white TV shows."

"Pretty much sums it up. But they're always a good time and an easy way to meet people in town."

She pointed toward the dunk tank as they started walking again. "I heard Grace talking about a dunk tank, but I still can't believe there's one over there."

No sooner did she say the words than a loud cheer came from the direction of the tank, a good sign someone had sent Drew into the water.

"I'm guessing Drew lives in town. Is he a friend of yours?"

Did she really not know who was in the tank? Drew McKenzie had attended Sean and Mia's wedding the previous fall. And although a newer addition to the friendly poker games, Drew and his wife had been attending them since the winter. It seemed unlikely that either Mia or Sean had never mentioned the guy in Angie's presence.

"He grew up in town and bought a house here over the winter. But with football season starting up, Drew and Kelsey plan to spend most of their time at his house in Weston because it's closer to the stadium."

Angie zipped in front of him faster than a bullet traveling through the barrel of his gun. "Drew McKenzie, the quarterback for the New England Rebels, is in there?" She pointed over her shoulder toward the center of the common.

HER SISTER often referred to friends named Drew and Kelsey, but nothing Mia said ever suggested the guy who joined their poker games was the famous quarterback. Maybe she should have put two and two together, because he had attended Mia and Sean's wedding. However, when she'd seen the well-known athlete having his picture taken outside the church with Nikki Reese, someone Mia had starred in several movies with, she'd assumed he was there as Nikki's date. The woman had a thing for professional athletes, especially football players. She'd dated at least two players from New England and one from Jacksonville.

"Yep. And I plan on sending him under the water tonight." Dakota's smile expressed how much he was looking forward to it.

She didn't have crushes anymore. She was simply too old for them. Except for when it came to Drew McKenzie, the quarterback who'd led his team to three consecutive championship wins. "Mia's mentioned his name and his wife's. I didn't realize she was talking about *him*."

A look of annoyance bordering on jealousy crossed Dakota's face, and she immediately regretted her tone. She was standing with a man she really liked and wanted to spend time with while acting like a teenager in love with her favorite musician. If he talked about Nikki Reese or someone she'd costarred with in a similar tone while out with her, she'd be mad as hell.

"I can introduce you to Drew when he gets out. He won't be in there all night."

Damage control time. "Don't worry about it. If we run into him, you can, but I don't want to waste our time trying to find him later."

His expression remained a bit skeptical, so she released his shoulders and put her hands on either side of his waist. "I'm looking forward to some time in the hot tub with you too much to spend all night here." She whispered the words against his ear before closing her lips around his earlobe and giving it a gentle tug.

Aware of the setting, she didn't linger. Instead, she moved back to his side and took his hand. "How do you feel about dancing?"

"Somewhat indifferent. But if you want to dance, I'll join you."

Angie surveyed the area. She enjoyed dancing but didn't love it, so at least for the moment, she felt no need to join the crowd on the dance floor. "Maybe later."

They skirted their way around the dance floor and past the bouncy houses. She'd loved them and trampolines as a child. If she joined the line to go inside, how many strange looks would she get? Probably too many, and she'd rather not call any attention to herself tonight. After the guide on the ghost tour asked for a picture with her, she'd worried someone in the group might recognize her and ask for an autograph or picture too.

She didn't want to worry tonight. Since it had worked the day she flew from California to Boston, she'd opted for an outfit similar to the one she'd worn then and skipped any makeup. In her opinion, dressed in denim shorts, an old Dartmouth College T-shirt, and a New England Rebels baseball cap, she looked like half the people at the block party. So unless she drew attention to herself, no one should see her and immediately recognize her.

As they got closer to the food area, her stomach rumbled. She didn't know what they were cooking on the large grills, but it smelled delicious. The meat wasn't the only thing she smelled. The aroma of popcorn mingled with it, as well as something else she couldn't identify.

She eyed the lines at the tables. "I'd suggest we get something to eat, but the lines are so long right now."

"Trust me, they won't get much shorter. If you're hungry, we can grab something to eat."

She was about to suggest they wait when someone walked by with a hamburger in one hand and a hot dog in the other. The sight and smell caused her stomach to protest twice as loud as before. "I'm suddenly starving."

Despite the long lines, it didn't take them long to get two

Italian sausage grinders, a bag of chips to share, and bottles of water.

Dakota stuffed his wallet back in his pocket and picked up the two paper plates. "I suggest you leave room for some of Mrs. Mitchell's homemade donuts."

When they'd passed by, she'd taken a quick glance at the dessert table, and while everything on it looked tasty, nothing jumped out as something she had to try tonight. Homemade donuts, however, sounded like a must before they left.

If she had to sit on the grass and eat, she would, but she kept an eye out for an empty table as they walked. She was about to give up when she spotted her brother-in-law and sister.

"Mia and Sean are here." She gestured toward their table.

"Just spotted them too."

Her sister noticed them before they reached the picnic table and waved. "I've been keeping an eye out for you," she said once Angie and Dakota reached them.

While Angie hadn't mentioned Dakota or their new relationship to Avery or Mom, she'd discussed its progression with Mia, so her sister had known they were coming together tonight.

Angie gave Mia a quick hug before hugging Sean, who had Natalie attached to him in a baby carrier. After dropping a kiss on her niece's head, she sat on the bench near Mia.

"Angie, you've met Sean's brother-in-law, Jake, but I don't know if you have, Dakota," Mia continued.

Like the man seated across the table needed an introduction. Jake Sherbrooke, the only biological son of President Warren Sherbrooke, had appeared on more tabloid covers and internet sites than she had, and that was saying a lot. Once dubbed Prince Charming, the media had portrayed him as a carefree playboy who did nothing but spend his family's money and sleep around. Angie knew how much the media loved to make up stories, so she had her doubts about whether or not any of it was true. Even if all the stories had been accurate, since Jake's marriage to Sean's sister and the birth of his son, the media spent much less time on him.

"And the handsome guy sitting next to Jake is his son, Garrett," Mia said.

The young boy looked just like his too-handsome-for-words father. It really was no wonder the paparazzi had loved photographing Jake. In sixteen or seventeen years, they'd love taking pictures of his son too.

At least from the way Mia spoke, Jake and Charlie rarely traveled apart. "Is Charlie here tonight?" The last time she saw Charlie had been at Mia's baby shower, and she wouldn't mind catching up with her.

"She went over to say hello to Mrs. Mitchell," Jake answered as he handed his son a covered plastic cup.

If Charlie was over talking to Mrs. Mitchell, it might be a long time before she returned. According to both Mia and Sean, the older widow loved to chat.

Sean raised his bottle of water to his lips but paused. "Hey, how did it go with the interior designer yesterday?"

After swallowing her mouthful of food, she wiped her mouth with a napkin. "I approved his designs for the kitchen and all the bathrooms. I should've sent him the pictures of your house sooner. Maybe they could've already started the work. As for the rest of the house, I've decided to leave everything as is and just have someone come in and paint." The longer she lived in the house, the more she loved it just the way it was—with the exception of the outdated kitchen and bathrooms.

"Did you buy a house in town?" Jake asked.

"Last month, but I only moved in about two weeks ago." Only two weeks might have passed, but she already considered North Salem home.

Jake broke his donut into several smaller pieces and added them to the paper plate in front of his son. "My cousin, Brett, moved to town a couple of weeks ago too. He's dancing with his girlfriend, but he'll be back at some point."

Charlie joined them moments before Jake's cousin and his cousin's date returned to the table. Unlike Jake and several of his other cousins, Brett Sherbrooke never showed up on the covers of tabloid magazines. And while most of the Sherbrooke cousins shared a strong family resemblance, no one would immediately recognize Brett as a member of the wealthy family. The only reason she recognized him tonight was because he was running in the special election to fill the empty Senate seat in Washington. And since his last name was Sherbrooke, his campaign was getting a huge amount of media attention.

Jake appeared ready to make introductions, but his cousin spoke first.

"Nice to see you again, Dakota." Brett extended his hand in Dakota's direction as he and his girlfriend sat.

"You've met?" Jake glanced from Brett to Dakota and then to his cousin again.

Brett put his arm affectionately over the shoulder of the attractive strawberry-blonde woman next to him. "Dakota lives across the street from me. He helped Mack and me get rid of the tree that came down during the storm."

One of the many newspaper articles she'd read about the campaign mentioned Brett was a North Salem resident, but she hadn't realized he was also Dakota's neighbor.

Jake sighed loud enough for everyone at the table to hear. "My condolences, Dakota, for having him as a neighbor. Actually, I should probably put something in the local paper offering the whole town my condolences."

Like a good political candidate, Brett ignored the barb and introduced Dakota and her to his girlfriend, Jennifer.

A friendly and sometimes boisterous conversation, one Natalie somehow managed to sleep through, continued for the next hour. Eventually, though, Mia slipped the backpack she used as a diaper bag over her shoulder and gave Angie a hug.

"Are you sure you guys don't want to come back to our house for a little while?"

Everyone else at the table was going back to Mia and Sean's house. While she loved spending time with her sister, brother-in-law, and especially her niece, she wanted some time alone with Dakota.

Perhaps she should get Dakota's opinion on the matter, but she wasn't going to. "Positive."

After a round of goodbyes, the three couples walked away, leaving them alone.

"If you wanted to go visit, I wouldn't have minded."

"I can spend time with Mia sometime next week." She trailed her fingertips over his hand and along the long white scar that stretched from his wrist to the middle of his forearm. "For the rest of the night, I just want to be with you. And unless you want to stay here, I'm ready to leave."

TEN

ALTHOUGH he never got a chance to send Drew into the water, when Angie said she was ready to leave, he didn't complain. As enjoyable as it'd been visiting with Sean and everyone else, during much of the conversation he kept envisioning Angie dressed in whatever swimsuit she'd packed, soaking wet. While he had a fantastic imagination, he knew the real deal would be so much better.

Dakota switched on the kitchen lights and tossed his keys and cell phone on the table. "Are you still leaning toward the hot tub, or would you rather go for a swim? It really doesn't matter to me."

Angie grabbed the oversized bag she'd left on the kitchen floor earlier and slipped the straps over her shoulder. "A swim sounds nice, but I think I'd rather relax in the hot tub tonight."

"Hot tub it is."

While she disappeared into the small bathroom off the hallway, he took the steps upstairs two at a time. With a little luck, he could beat her outside and be in the hot tub before she got out there, because no bathing suit was going to hide the erection his untucked T-shirt was covering at the moment.

As a general rule, he liked his house kept neat and tidy. Tonight he left his clothes in a pile on the bedroom floor before turning off the light and heading back downstairs. The bathroom door was still closed, and he knocked on it rather than walk by. "I'll meet you outside."

The previous owners had installed both bright spotlights in the backyard as well as softer lights designed to provide a relaxing atmosphere rather than light up an entire city block. He usually opted for the brighter lights when he was out back. Tonight, he turned on the other ones instead. After uncovering the hot tub, he switched on the jets and stepped inside.

Tipping his head back, he studied the star-filled sky. He'd never been good at identifying the constellations. Usually the only two he could find were Orion's Belt and the Big Dipper. Tonight he didn't recognize any, but it was still a beautiful sight.

But nothing like the sight he caught when he looked over toward the door. He'd known the vision provided by his imagination wouldn't do Angie justice, but he hadn't realized just how lacking it would be. Swallowing, he wondered if there was any steam coming from his ears as he watched her walk his way.

The doll clothes he'd seen in stores contained more fabric than the dark purple string bikini Angie wore. When she'd worn the snug tank top earlier in the week, he judged her breasts to be about a C cup. The barely there top revealed he'd been off by a size.

Dakota tore his eyes away from her breasts for the moment and let them travel lower. An amethyst stud glittered in her navel, but the gemstone wasn't what really caught his attention. Nope, the exotic-looking flower tattoo to the right and slightly lower than her navel did. Her bikini bottoms covered part of it, and he wondered just how much farther down it went.

She took her time stepping into the hot tub and lowering herself into the water next to him. "The water's perfect."

He disagreed. Before she'd come outside, it'd been great; now he felt like was sitting in a pot of boiling water.

Under the water, she took his hand and held it against her thigh. "I'm glad we went to the party. I had fun." She kissed the side of his neck. "But I've been looking forward to this since you picked me up."

Releasing his hand, she ran her finger across his thigh until she reached the junction of his leg and torso.

Actions spoke louder than words, so rather than share his thoughts, Dakota set about showing her. When his lips came down on hers, he didn't need to tease them apart. They opened willingly, her tongue tangling with his.

While their mouths made love, he reached out, intent on putting his arms around her. She didn't give him the chance. In one swift motion, she straddled his lap and moved against him, sending pleasure like he'd never experienced through his entire body.

Only when he needed air did he pull his mouth away and switch his attention to the pulse in her neck. After kissing it, he moved his lips across her shoulder until they met the thin bikini strap. Dakota hooked a finger under the fabric and pushed it away. Once the strap was no longer in his way, he pressed his lips against her bare skin and made a trail back toward her neck. Then he transferred his attention to her other side, intending to repeat what he'd just done.

Angie stopped him before he could.

The hands that had been caressing his upper back under the water stopped, and she leaned back, putting a few inches between them. She didn't say a word. Instead, she met his eyes and reached behind her for the bikini's strings. No longer tied around her, the top floated up as she slipped both arms out of it.

He didn't require any further permission. Cupping her breasts, he flicked his thumb against an already taut nipple.

With a groan, she moved against him one more time before raising herself enough so his lips could replace his thumb. Her skin was warm and wet from the water, and he lavished one breast with attention. Ready to treat the other to the same, he switched sides. Dakota licked away the water clinging to her nipple and then closed his lips around it. Angie didn't give him a chance to linger. Instead, she pulled away and settled herself back on the bench next to him before he could do anything more.

Momentarily confused, he started to ask if something was wrong. The hand sliding past his waistband and touching him stopped the question from exiting his mouth.

"Hell yeah."

Her smile told him he'd spoken the words aloud. The hand not giving him pleasure reached for his. She brought it to her chest before moving it lower over her breast and stomach, all while touching him. The stud in her navel brushed against his palm, and he stopped breathing as he waited, wondering if she'd continue the path south.

He didn't have to wonder for long. Angie moved his hand under the fabric and didn't stop again until his fingers settled between her open legs. Much like when she took off her top, he got the message loud and clear.

Dakota took his time teasing her, and she certainly repaid the favor.

"Did you bring any protection out with you?" She sounded like she'd not only run the Boston Marathon but also set a new record while doing it.

Damn, he wished he had. "Nope." He didn't sound much

better.

"We'll both have to remember for next time." Angie's hand released him and moved up toward his torso. "Do you have any inside? If not, I have some in my bag."

He didn't have a lot, but he had one or two condoms in his room. "Upstairs."

ANGIE WATCHED Dakota walk back in the kitchen and switch off the lights outside. He'd gone out to cover the hot tub and turn off the jets, two things they'd been far too preoccupied to do earlier.

Her eyes followed him as he crossed to the refrigerator. Before coming downstairs, he'd pulled on his jeans but hadn't bothered with a T-shirt. He'd been in the hot tub already when she'd gone outside, so she hadn't gotten a great view of what his T-shirts covered. For the trip upstairs, her lips were locked with his, and once in Dakota's bedroom, he hadn't bothered to turn the lights on before they landed on his bed. They hadn't bothered to pull the blankets back either.

But now in the well-lit kitchen, she could enjoy the view of him shirtless.

"We've got pistachio, cookie dough, vanilla bean, Dutch chocolate, strawberry, and peanut butter cup." After listing the ice cream flavors in the freezer, he glanced over at her.

"Either you're running an ice cream parlor out of your house, or you have an ice cream problem."

"Ice cream is a weakness of mine. Especially when I'm sick." Although she hadn't answered him, he took each of the containers from the freezer and placed them on the table. "About three weeks ago, I was sick as a dog with a nasty cold and strep. Even missed two days of work. For four or five days, I ate nothing but ice cream and pizza."

If ice cream was something he indulged in often, it certainly didn't show. "Carbs are my biggest weakness. It doesn't matter what kind. If I could get everything I needed from them, I'd never eat another vegetable or piece of meat."

Back at the refrigerator, he grabbed a can of whipped cream and a jar of hot fudge. After popping the jar into the microwave, he came back to the table with a couple of bowls, two spoons, and a stack of napkins. "It won't be the same as homemade donuts, but we have everything to make sundaes except for walnuts. I finished the bag the other morning."

Although it'd been their intention to get donuts, they never made it back to the food tables before leaving the block party. "I'm not a fan of walnuts anyway." She'd tolerate them in brownies and banana bread if she had to, but they never got added to anything else she ate, including sundaes.

Angie added a few scoops of both chocolate and vanilla ice cream to a bowl. "I'm sorry you didn't get a chance to dunk Drew before we left."

He piled a little of each flavor into his bowl and then poured some of the hot fudge over the ice cream. "Judging by all the cheering, plenty of other people sent him into the water. I'll just clean out his wallet next time he shows up for a poker game instead. I'll enjoy doing that even more than I would've enjoyed sending him into the water."

Once she'd covered her ice cream with a generous helping of hot fudge and whipped cream, she took her first spoonful. Whether it was because it'd been so long since she last ate ice cream or what, the flavors tasted amazing. "Where did you get this?" There was no brand name on the containers; only the flavor inside was printed on the labels.

"Drummonds. It's a small place in Marblehead. They make all their own ice cream. If I can't make it over there, I settle for what's at the store, but I was out that way right before I got sick and stocked up." A sundae twice the size of hers sat in front of him, but Dakota didn't dig in. "I'm going to put this away so it doesn't melt, but if you want more, let me know."

When she finished what was in her bowl, she wanted more of something, but it wasn't ice cream. They'd used the two condoms in his bedroom, but she had two more in her bag. She intended on using at least one of them tonight, which was why she'd only bothered to pull on her T-shirt before they came down.

Back at the table, he dug into his dessert, and neither said anything for a few minutes. Honestly, Angie didn't mind. It gave her a chance to indulge her sweet tooth and study her dessert companion more.

"Have you met Ella and Striker?" He paused in the process of scooping up more of his sundae.

"Only Ella. She was at Mia's baby shower."

"Next weekend they're getting married. It's short notice, but will you come with me?"

She'd gone to Mia and Sean's wedding because it was her sister, but these days she tended to avoid weddings unless they were for celebrities. She'd even skipped her aunt's last year. It wasn't because she considered herself too good for them. Rather, it was because she remembered all too well what happened at her older cousin John's wedding six years ago. John and his fiancée spent two years planning their wedding and invited everyone, even the youngest members of their families. Somehow the media got wind of the fact that Mia Troy would be attending a wedding at the First Congregational Church in Woodlawn, Massachusetts. Photographers and TV crews descended on the small town and turned their cousin's wedding into a circus. Mia had felt terrible afterward. John and his wife hadn't been too pleased either.

Rather than cause a similar incident, Angie stopped

attending family events such as weddings and retirement parties after landing her first major movie role.

But it might be safe to attend this wedding. She'd been in town for two weeks already, and she hadn't seen a single photographer. "They won't mind a last-minute guest?" The facility where Mia and Sean held their reception had required a final guest count long before the day of the event.

"When I mailed in my RSVP, I planned on bringing a friend. Christine works on my squad. Last year she needed a date to a wedding and I went with her. But she canceled on me last month after she started seeing Nadine, an analyst in the building. Nadine's parents are celebrating their fiftieth wedding anniversary this month, and she wants Christine to come to the surprise party planned for them next weekend." Dakota ate another spoonful of his sundae, but this time a little whipped cream got left behind on his mouth.

"Then count me in." Leaning closer, she licked the cream off his lips before giving him a kiss intended to let him know she'd had enough dessert for now and was ready for something else.

Catching on quickly, Dakota tugged her to her feet and slipped his hands under her Dartmouth College T-shirt as they started down the hall.

When they approached the bathroom, she ended their kiss and popped inside to grab the bag she'd left on the floor. Dakota's lips came down on hers again the moment she exited the room. His mouth didn't leave hers again until they both fell onto his bed.

AFTER STRETCHING, Angie moved onto her side and threw an arm over Dakota's waist. "I have no idea what time it is, do you?"

He glanced at his watch, the only thing currently on his body besides her. Whatever blankets were usually on the bed were now on the floor, along with his jeans and her T-shirt. "Almost midnight." Instead of tucking the arm behind his head again, he touched her hand resting his stomach. "Do you want me to drive you home?"

It'd been at least a year since she'd woken up in the morning with a man. Her last boyfriend had never stayed the night at her place, and she'd never wanted to stay at his. Tonight she didn't want to stay anywhere but Dakota's bed. "I'd rather stay."

"Good, because I want you here." Rolling from the bed, he collected the blankets from the floor. "If you want something to sleep in, I can get you a T-shirt."

She often slept naked at home and simply added extra blankets if she got cold. Dakota gave off enough body heat that she wouldn't need to worry about getting chilly tonight. "Nah, I prefer sleeping like this. But if I get cold, I'll use you as my personal heater."

He tossed the blankets back on the bed before climbing in and pulling her close. "What are your plans for tomorrow?"

"Nothing specific." She fought to stifle a yawn. Until a few moments ago, she'd been wide awake, but now her eyes didn't want to stay open.

Next to her, Dakota yawned too. "I want to stop at the hospital and see Jessie and Mack. But afterward I was thinking about going for a hike. Do you want to come?"

The last time she'd gone on a hike, she'd been seven years old. Her Girl Scout troop had gone on a nature hike to earn one of their badges. Angie remembered enjoying the excursion, but it could've been because she'd been with some of her closest friends.

"Sure, I'll give it a try." She didn't try to fight the next yawn as her eyes drifted closed.

ELEVEN

WITH THE WHOLE weekend off from both jobs, Shane had driven up to the Mount Washington area Friday night and checked into a motel. Then yesterday he'd met Cathy, the local real estate agent helping him find a house. They'd spent much of the day looking at homes. Some he'd found listed on the internet, and others Cathy thought he'd be interested in. Of the eight they'd looked at, only one had come close to being right, and it had been slightly out of the price range he hoped to stay in. Between working two jobs and the inheritance his grandparents left him when they passed away, he had a decent amount saved. If he had to use all of it for a down payment, he would. Shane wanted their home to be perfect, but if possible, he'd rather avoid emptying his savings account completely while still having a low mortgage.

This morning after checking out of the motel and grabbing a quick breakfast at a local mom-and-pop restaurant, he met Cathy at her office again for another day of house hunting. So far they'd seen two. The first he'd crossed off his list the moment they pulled into the driveway. Whoever had taken the photos of the house had done some Photoshop magic or something, because the house and property barely resembled what he'd seen on the real estate site. The second home had been nice. It had a decent view of the mountains, something he most definitely wanted, but the closet in his current bedroom was bigger than the home's second bedroom. When they had children, he didn't want their son or daughter getting claustrophobic every time they went to bed. Ideally, he wanted a bigger yard as well. It didn't need to be the size of a football field or anything, but he wanted enough land to set up a swing set and maybe a pool while still having some open space.

"I know you wanted something in Conway or Albany, but when this listing came up, I immediately thought of you." Cathy glanced at him before turning her attention back to the road.

He'd picked Conway because Door2Door Express had a distribution center located there. He'd already looked into what he needed to do so he could work out of the center up here instead of the one out of Danvers. He'd also put Conway at the top of his list of towns because it was a popular tourist spot. In the winter people came up to ski and snowmobile. In the warmer months, tourists visited to go camping and hiking. With so many people coming to visit, the area had numerous restaurants. If he wanted to earn a little extra money waiting tables, he'd be able to find a second job without any trouble.

When they passed a sign welcoming them to Jefferson, New Hampshire, Shane checked his watch. It had taken them an hour and fifteen minutes to get from the property in Conway to the town. He'd prefer a shorter commute to and from work every day, but he considered anything less than two hours manageable, especially if there wasn't traffic. Regardless of the time or the day of the week, there shouldn't be too much traffic between Conway and Jefferson.

The real estate agent turned left onto a dirt road with no street sign. Trees stretched out on both sides of the road. As far as Shane could tell, there were no driveways cutting through the forest, and he didn't see any homes.

"There are only two houses on this road." She pointed toward the mailbox with a large B on it located at the end of the road. "Josh and Gina Bettencourt live up there. I graduated with Josh. They're both friendly, and they have two children in elementary school."

He didn't plan on getting to know any of his neighbors, so whether or not they were friendly didn't matter to him.

Cathy turned right and continued up a long narrow driveway surrounded on both sides by trees. "Josh's brother Teddy and his wife own this house."

She stopped in front of a log cabin-style home. A wide porch ran across the front of the house. A large floral wreath hung on the front door, and it matched the flowers in the planters set out on the porch. Off to one side, a large wooden swing set stood along with a green turtle-shaped sandbox and a trampoline.

"How many acres is the property?" As far as he could tell, there wasn't any fencing to indicate where the property ended. In fact, all he saw were trees and the tops of the mountains in the distance, and all he heard were birds.

After removing the key from the lockbox, Cathy checked the listing in her hand. "Four and a half acres, and the property borders conservation land, so you won't have to worry about any new constructions going in."

So far everything about this place was perfect.

The front door opened into a large living room. An enormous stone fireplace occupied much of one wall, and he could see another door leading out to the backyard. A staircase hugged the wall leading up to the second level.

"The smallest of the three bedrooms is downstairs." Cathy

walked through the living room toward the kitchen. "There's a half bathroom down here and two full bathrooms upstairs."

He checked out the kitchen and the finished basement before heading upstairs. The walls in the master bedroom were a horrible light green, and a matching area rug covered the floor. But it was easy to change paint colors and replace area rugs. Before leaving the room, he peeked into the master bathroom. The whirlpool bathtub almost made up for the dreadful paint color on the walls in here too. But again, painting was easy and, if he did it himself, inexpensive.

Shane passed by the bathroom in the hallway and opened the last door. Unlike the other room, this one was painted blue and various dinosaurs were stuck to the walls. The comforters covering the two twin beds in the room also contained dinosaurs, and over each bed was a wall plaque with a boy's name on it. Plenty of natural light came in through both the windows and the skylight in the ceiling. Some new paint and this room would make an ideal nursery.

"Are you ready to look around outside?"

"I don't need to. You were right, this house is perfect. I want to make an offer on it."

"Excellent. Let's go back to my office, and we can complete the necessary paperwork."

He glanced around a final time before walking back into the hall.

It'd taken some searching, but he was one step closer. Soon he and Angie could leave North Salem behind for good.

LOCATED about a mile from the high school, the North Salem Historical Society occupied what had once been the public library before the town constructed a new one fifteen years ago. Since the historical society was a nonprofit organization, the building didn't have employees. Instead, volunteers maintained the collections and the organization's website. The same volunteers conducted various programs, including ones on the history of North Salem as well as on tracing back your genealogy. With no employees, the building wasn't open on a set schedule. Anyone interested in viewing the collections needed to contact Renee Adams, the secretary of the historical society, and set up an appointment. Angie reached out to the secretary right after finding the hidden room in her house. Once she had the appointment for today, she invited Mia along. As Angie expected, her sister had jumped at the chance to get inside and do some research.

Pulling in next to the only vehicle in the lot, Angie put the car in Park.

"When I asked Maureen to watch Natalie today, she mentioned the historical society has documents dating back to when the town was founded in 1680." Excitement vibrated in Mia's voice as she collected her purse off the floor and opened the car door.

With no idea how long they'd be here, Mia had asked her mother-in-law to watch Natalie. Today was actually the first time her sister had left Natalie with anyone other than Sean, and Angie expected Mia to either call or text Maureen several times while they were here.

"According to her, Evelyn Abbott's ancestors were some of the first settlers here. Evelyn is the president of the historical society, and if not for her, the organization wouldn't exist." Her sister exited the car before Angie unplugged her cell phone.

With a slight groan, Angie stepped out. Although the intensity of her workouts varied depending on whether or not she was getting ready for a role, she exercised on a regular basis. Despite the hours in the gym, yesterday's hike with Dakota had kicked her butt.

"Are you limping?" Mia had seen her pull up to the house, and she'd come right out before Angie got out of her car.

Angie nodded as she dropped her keys in her purse. "Muscles I didn't even know I had hurt today." She'd felt more like a hundred-year-old woman when she climbed out of bed this morning. And forget about getting down the stairs to the kitchen. Her hamstrings had burned with each step she took.

"Do I want to know why?"

By the time Dakota dropped her off last night, it had been too late to call Mia and give her sister a rundown of her weekend.

Climbing the steps to the door, she groaned again. "After we stopped at the hospital to visit Jessie and Mack yesterday, Dakota and I went hiking. I was okay until near the end, and then my legs got a little tired. But I wasn't expecting to be this sore today."

An older woman with tight silver curls greeted them when they walked in the building, putting an end to their personal conversation for the moment. Although she'd never met the woman, she remembered seeing her seated next to Mrs. Mitchell at the block party.

"Welcome." Lips covered in coral-colored lipstick formed a smile as she extended her hand. "I'm June Martin, the historical society's treasurer. Renee asked me to fill in for her today. She came down with some kind of stomach bug last night." Her voice contained the same Bostonian accent shared by everyone who'd grown up in the area.

June Martin appeared fragile, but her handshake told a different story. "I'm Angie, and this is my sister Mia."

Releasing her hand, June turned her full attention Mia's way. "It's nice to see you again. Maureen showed me pictures of Natalie last week at our bridge game. She's beautiful. Is Maureen watching her this morning?"

Mia answered a few more questions before June seemed to remember why they were there. "When I spoke with Renee, she mentioned you're looking for information about the home you recently purchased. Is there anything specific you want to know, or are you looking for general facts?"

"Specific. At the moment, all I know is the home was built in 1820 by Roger Franklin." The historical registry plaque on the front of the home provided her with the basic information. "But I found something that makes me think the house might have been a stop on the Underground Railroad."

"Really? Do you mind telling me what you found?" June's face lit up with excitement. She was obviously a history buff like Mia.

"Behind what appears to be a built-in bookcase is a ladder. It leads up to a small windowless room in the attic. And the ladder is the only way to access it." After finding the room, she'd gone up to the attic, but there was no door leading into the small room. In fact, nothing about the attic indicated the room even existed.

"Well, I definitely know of one home that was part of the underground here in town. It's located on Blackthorne Road. There are also a few known stops in Salem, so it's a possibility. We have a considerable amount of information on Roger Franklin downstairs. To date, he's the only North Salem resident to serve in the United States Senate. Hopefully, Brett Sherbrooke will win the upcoming election and change that for us."

The historical society's treasurer led them downstairs and provided them with additional facts regarding Roger Franklin, including whom he'd married, where he'd gone to school, how many children he'd had, and when he'd passed away. "As far as I know, Roger never made his feelings on slavery public, so I cannot say for certain if he was for or against it. But I do know his eldest son, Nathan, was an attorney like his father and involved in the abolitionist movement."

"What about his other children?" Mia pulled her cell phone from a pocket and checked the screen, no doubt looking for a text from Maureen, before shoving it back.

Switching on lights, June escorted them into a room filled with bookcases and maps. Old pictures of the town hung on the walls, and there were two worktables in the center of the room.

"Ida, his oldest daughter, married Patrick Milford, who later went on to be elected mayor of Boston. Neither of them publicly spoke about slavery. His younger son, George, worked as a Union doctor during the Civil War. After the war, he taught at Harvard. Roger's youngest child, Martha, was involved in the women's suffrage movement."

June Martin was better than any internet site or encyclopedia.

"We have every book and map the library owns listed in the computer database. Many of North Salem's official records have also been reproduced in digital format. You can access them either here or at home via our website." She gestured toward the older-style desktop computer set up near the far wall. "If you need any help, I'll be upstairs in the office. I have plenty of work to keep me busy for hours, so take your time today. And if you learn your home was part of the Underground Railroad, please let me know."

Mia didn't wait to get down to work. She dropped her purse on the table and went straight to the computer before June left the room. As she typed, she moved their conversation back to where it'd been before June greeted them upstairs. "Sean and I stopped in to see Jessie yesterday too. She didn't mention that you and Dakota came in."

Angie dragged a chair over to the computer and sat.

Randomly pulling books off the shelves would be a waste of time, and with only one computer in the room, she couldn't help her sister search the database. "We went early, not long after we got up."

"We got up?" Mia looked away from the computer screen and in her direction. "Does that mean you guys had a sleep-over after the block party?"

Whether it was because they were close in age or simply had similar personalities, they'd never kept things from each other. And while she might not share the details of her new relationship with Avery, she saw no reason not to share even some of the more intimate ones with Mia.

"I spent Saturday night at Dakota's. Sunday we stopped at my house long enough for me to shower and change before heading over to the hospital. Then we went straight from there to Wachusett Mountain."

"Sean and I have ridden his Harley up to the top of the mountain, but we've never hiked." Mia turned her attention back to her search results. She jotted down the names and call numbers of several books and handed the list to her before writing down the information for five or six different books on another sheet of paper. "You work on finding those and I'll locate this group."

She'd never liked searching for nonfiction books in the library. Fiction books were easy as long as you knew the author's last name, but she found using call numbers to track down books difficult. Mia, however, had no problem finding the titles on her list.

"I'm glad things are going well between you guys. I like Dakota a lot."

Angie found the last item on her list, a book titled *A History of the Franklin Family of Massachusetts,* and joined Mia at a worktable.

"Do you guys have plans this week?" Mia didn't bother to look up from what she was reading.

If she hoped to find any useful information, she'd have to follow her sister's lead, which meant talking and reading at the same time. "Nothing concrete except Ella and Striker's wedding on Saturday. Do you have a dress I can borrow?" She owned plenty of dresses appropriate for a wedding, but they were all still in California. With no special events on her calendar, she'd seen no reason to pack any of them.

"I have a few possibilities. You can check them out when you bring me home. If you don't like any of them, Natalie and I can go shopping with you this week."

"Even if I find something in your closet, let's plan to go shopping this week. So far I've done a terrible job of spoiling my niece."

"Believe me, she isn't lacking for anything. Maureen brings her something new almost every time she visits. Charlie isn't much better."

Neither spoke again for quite some time as they pored through the various books and old records stored inside the building.

Leaning back in her chair, Angie rubbed her eyes. She'd just finished scanning the last book in her pile, *North Salem in the Nineteenth Century*. No specific locations were listed, but the book mentioned three homes in the town were well known by the conductors helping slaves escape to Canada. "I think my eyes hurt more than my legs now."

"Wimp," Mia called from across the room. After not finding anything useful in the books, she'd gone back to the computer to search the various digital documents.

"Some of us don't spend hours reading history text-books." After relocating back to Massachusetts, Mia had returned to Harvard to finish the history degree she'd started years earlier.

"Actually, I'm getting a little tired too. It's way past the time for my afternoon coffee. And I'm hungry. Maybe we should take a break and grab some lunch. We can go through more of these records at my house after we eat, or I can do it when Natalie's taking a nap."

A caffeine pick-me-up and a hot lunch would hit the spot.

The historical society's treasurer looked up from her work when Angie tapped on the office door. "We're all set for today. Thank you for letting us in."

June removed the reading glasses from her face and set them on the desk. "Anytime. Did you find anything useful?"

"Possibly. According to one book downstairs, three homes in town were known stops for those heading toward Canada. And the public records show that when Roger Franklin moved to Washington to serve in the Senate, he sold my home to his eldest son. It seems plausible that once Nathan owned the home, he had the hidden room in the attic constructed."

"I agree. From the little I've read about Nathan Franklin, it sounds like something he would do. Feel free to say no, but could I come by sometime and see the room you found? I find the nineteenth century fascinating. When I taught history at the high school, it was my favorite time period."

Back in California, if someone she barely knew asked to come and look around her house, she'd refuse in the blink of an eye. But this wasn't Los Angeles. "Sure. How does this Wednesday or Thursday around one o'clock sound?"

"Wednesday at one sounds great. I'll see you then."

With the sun shining and not a cloud in sight, it was the perfect day for a convertible. Even though she didn't expect them to be in the car long, Angie put the top down as soon as she got behind the wheel.

"Do you want to eat at my house or go out?"

As long as she didn't have to do any reading, she didn't care where they went for lunch. "Either is fine with me."

"Let's go—" Mia's ringing cell phone cut off the rest of her sentence. Neither of their devices had made a sound all day. Their silence hadn't stopped Mia from checking hers numerous times. "It's Avery," she said, checking the screen.

Angie waited and listened to Mia's half of the conversation.

"Okay, Angie and I will be home in a few minutes." Mia put the phone away and looked her way. "Did you know Avery was coming?"

"I haven't talked to her in over a week." Their last conversation had been the day she and Dakota went on the ghost tour. Although she'd made her feelings clear, Angie had expected Avery to call back by now to once again try to change her mind. If she was in North Salem, did it mean she'd decided to try persuading her in person?

"Well, she's waiting for us at my house."

"Is Mom with her?"

Mom wasn't supposed to visit until October, and by then she'd be ready for a houseguest. Right now she wasn't even close. The bathrooms hadn't been remodeled, and she only had one bed in the house. If Mom had come with Avery, she'd insist on staying with Mia and Sean, and there wasn't a thing she could do to change the situation except give up her own bedroom and sleep on the sofa.

"She didn't mention her, but I hope not."

For Sean's sake, Angie did too.

Only Avery sat inside the black sports car when they pulled into Mia's driveway. Simultaneously, they both sighed and glanced at each other. "She's alone," Angie whispered before she opened her door.

Maureen and Max greeted them when they walked in the house. After filling Mia in on when Natalie last ate and what time she went down for her nap, she gathered up her things. "Be sure to call me if you need anything." Maureen gave Mia a motherly hug and a kiss on the cheek then headed out.

Mia locked the front door and turned to face Avery. "Angie and I are going to eat lunch. Are you hungry?"

"A little." Never a big fan of dogs, Avery gave Max a wide berth and followed them toward the kitchen. "I haven't had anything since my smoothie at the airport this morning."

Before Avery started with her lecture about what a mistake she was making by moving, Angie better start a conversation about something else. "Why didn't you tell us you were coming?"

"It was a last-minute decision. Since you two seem to love North Salem so much, I decided to spend some time here and see what's so great about it."

Angie didn't care for the condescending tone Avery used when she mentioned North Salem, but it was better than the you're-being-an-idiot tone she'd used during their last conversation.

"And I wanted to meet Natalie." When Natalie was born, Avery had been in Rome with Angie. While technically her sister could've flown back to the United States—she worked for Angie, not the studio—she decided to stay in Italy until Angie left.

"It's good to see you." Mia gave Avery another hug before starting on lunch.

"While I waited for you, I talked to Gram. I'm going to visit her and Pop on Saturday. She'd love it if you'd both come. I called Nana too, but she's visiting Sylvia in Texas."

Many of their cousins remained in Woodlawn where both of Angie's parents had grown up, though a few had left the area for different reasons. Their cousin Sylvia had attended college in Texas and after graduation decided to stay there.

"Sean and I have a wedding to go to this weekend." A soft

cry came from the baby video monitor on the counter. "Be right back."

Angie was still learning her way around a kitchen, but she could finish the salad Mia had started. After drying the cucumbers her sister washed, she sliced them and added them to the bowl of fresh spinach.

"Do you have plans? Gram promised to bake peanut butter cookies."

No one made peanut butter cookies like Gram. She could eat an entire batch by herself. "I'm going to the same wedding as Mia." The cherry tomatoes went in next, followed by a generous helping of feta cheese.

"Who do you know in town well enough to go to their wedding?"

She'd spent far more time in North Salem than her sister since Mia moved there, but Avery was right. Other than their sister and their brother-in-law, she didn't know anyone well enough to get invited to his or her wedding.

"Dakota asked me to go with him. You might've met him at Sean and Mia's wedding." Avery had spent most of the reception visiting with family members she hadn't seen in a long time rather than socializing with any of Mia's new friends.

Avery groaned. "Not you too."

Salad forgotten, Angie faced her older sister and crossed her arms. "What's that supposed to mean?"

"Mia gave up everything for a small-town guy. Don't get me wrong, I like Sean, but she gave up her career to be with him. When you bought the house here, I really thought you'd get bored in a few months and come back to California. I didn't think you'd get involved with someone while you were here."

Angie quickly checked the baby monitor. She didn't want Mia walking in on this particular conversation. At the moment, the monitor showed Mia and Natalie were still in the nursery. "First of all, Mia didn't give up anything. She'd been thinking about a change long before she met Sean—a man who treats her like a queen, by the way. And I told you back in the spring I wasn't taking on any new projects for the indefinite future. You, Mom, and Skylar just chose not to listen as usual."

"I never said Sean didn't treat her well. But Mia could've married someone who understood how important her career was to her instead of asking her to live here with him."

There was no point in trying to convince Avery she was wrong. In her mind, Sean was the reason Mia stopped acting, end of story.

"Yesterday, I ran into Anderson Brady. He's willing to do the sequel but only if you are."

Less than half an hour of conversation and already Avery was talking about the movie sequel again. Thankfully, Mia and Natalie's arrival put a temporary halt to it.

Angie's first instinct was to ask to hold Natalie. But this was Avery's first time seeing their niece, so she held her tongue.

Avery touched Natalie's hand. "I think she looks like you. Except for her eyes. Those look like Sean's."

"Do you want to hold her?"

Indecision crossed Avery's face, and she pulled her hand away. "I don't know. She's so tiny. I don't want to hurt her."

"Trust me, you won't break her." Mia settled Natalie in Avery's arm. "See, it's easy." She started a pot of coffee and then added grilled chicken to the ingredients on the counter so Angie could finish putting the salad together. "Did Angie tell you she's seeing someone?"

They glanced at each other and then Avery nodded. "She didn't get a chance to give me any juicy details."

She'd give her older sister all the juicy details she wanted if it meant Avery didn't bring up her career or the project with Anderson again.

"Honestly, she hasn't given me many either." Mia nudged her in the side before walking away with a stack of plates. "She can share them with both of us now."

TWELVE

DAKOTA PINCHED the bridge of his nose and shut his eyes. Most days he loved his job, but there were a few that had him wishing he still worked in the private sector. Thankfully, those days were far and few between. Today had been one of them though.

Perhaps that wasn't completely accurate. The first part of the day had been fine. He'd used the office gym for his morning workout and then met with his supervisor regarding one of his cases. Later he and Christine met a source they were working with for lunch. It was his meeting later in the afternoon that sent his day downhill. Something he'd expected, because so far all the meetings he'd had with this particular lawyer from the US attorney's office in Boston had put him in a foul mood. Except for a handful of lawyers, most of the ones he'd met who worked for the Department of Justice rubbed him the wrong way.

Robert E. Hewson III took it to an entirely different level. The man embodied every stereotype that existed regarding lawyers. He was far more concerned about his career and achieving his end goal, the office of attorney general, than anything else.

Dakota had returned from his meeting with Hewson two hours ago and had been working on paperwork ever since. People outside the agency might not realize it, but the job entailed a lot of paperwork. Not long after he'd started with the Bureau, Mom had asked how he liked it. He'd jokingly told her they should rename the agency the Federal Bureau of Investigation and Paperwork.

Opening his eyes, he pulled out the bottle of ibuprofen he kept in his desk and swallowed two. Then he turned his full attention back to the document on the computer. Once he finished this up, he could call it a night and finally go home.

"When I went up to the gym and you weren't here, I figured you'd left for the night," Jared Saunders, another agent on the squad, greeted. He dropped his gym bag near his desk and pulled his chair over to Dakota's side of the cubicle they shared.

Slightly older than him, Jared was one of the first friends he'd made in the Boston office when he transferred from Albany. "I had a meeting over at the US attorney's office late this afternoon."

"Judging by the sound of your voice, it was with Hewson." No one in the office liked dealing with the man.

Dakota nodded. "What are you still doing here?" Jared had a wife and four children, so unless impossible he tried to leave the office no later than six each night.

"Marissa took Lila and JT to a parks and rec sponsored event at the elementary school. Isabella is away at Girl Scout camp for the week, and Rachel's working. Since no one is home waiting for me, I decided to get in the workout I missed this morning."

It wasn't possible Rachel was old enough to work. Wasn't she still in middle school? "Rachel's working?"

"She turned sixteen back in March, and she'll be getting her driver's license in another few weeks."

"Thanks for the warning." He'd been in the Boston office for three years, but it still seemed impossible that Jared's oldest was already in high school and driving. "I can't believe she's sixteen."

"It goes by fast. Isabella is going into eighth grade, and JT is starting middle school. And this is Lila's last year at the elementary school. Wait, you'll see what I mean someday."

The sound of a cowbell alerted Jared to a new text message, and he unclipped his cell phone from his belt. After checking it, he typed back a reply and then looked at Dakota. "Marissa just sent me a picture. She wants to know if this is you."

Dakota accepted the device and glanced at the screen, expecting to see some silly cartoon character or maybe a funny GIF. Marissa was a jokester and enjoyed giving him a hard time whenever they all got together. Instead, it was a picture of him and Angie at the block party Saturday night. He hadn't seen anyone with cameras there, but just about everyone owned a cell phone. Hell, even Mrs. Mitchell owned a cell phone. And regardless of the type, they all had cameras in them.

"Where did Marissa get this?" He examined the picture. The edge of the dunk tank was visible in the photo, giving him a general idea of where they'd been standing when it was taken.

"Rachel sent it to her. And Rachel got it from a friend she works with." Taking the phone back, Jared glanced at the screen again. "Is that you and Angelina Troy?"

He didn't have a presence on social media. He saw no need for one. When he had news he wanted to share with family and friends, he either called them or sent them a text message. Most people weren't like him though. Especially teenagers. If a friend had sent this picture to Jared's daughter, it was possible she or he had either posted it on a social media site or found it on one. Either way, if this picture existed, several others had probably seen it.

"Yeah, Angie moved to North Salem. Her sister Mia lives there."

Recognition dawned on Jared's face. "That's right. I remember both you and Mack telling me Mia Troy is married to a friend of yours. Was this taken recently?"

"Over the weekend. We went to the town block party on Saturday night. Did Rachel tell Marissa if her friend took it or found it somewhere?"

"No, but I can ask."

Dakota checked his email for any messages while Jared sent texts to both his wife and daughter. If Rachel's friend found the picture on the internet, it was possible Angie had as well. They hadn't talked about it, but she must have accounts with all the social media sites. Even if she hadn't found it on one, the media might have and posted it on their own websites for the world to see.

The cowbell rang again, and Jared glanced at the device in his hand. "According to Rachel, her friend's older sister took the picture at the block party."

Well, that didn't help much. People had come and gone from the party all night, and most of them he didn't know. Not only that, it meant at least five people now had a copy of the picture. If it weren't on the internet yet, it soon would be.

"Do you want me to ask for the sister's name?"

He'd like to know who took the picture, but even if he knew, there wasn't anything he could do about it. "Nah, don't worry about it."

"If you change your mind, let me know. I'm heading out. See you tomorrow." Jared moved his chair back to his desk. The cowbell chimed again before he left, and he paused long enough to send another message before walking away.

It took Dakota another fifteen minutes to finish what he was working on. Before leaving he sent off a text message of his own asking Angie to call him when she got a chance. He wanted to ask if she'd seen any photos, and he was also curious about what she'd learned at the historical society today. Instead of a phone call, he got a message back.

Still at Mia's. Avery is here too. If I get home before ten, I'll call you.

He wasn't shocked she was still at her sister's house. The fact that Avery was there as well surprised him. Angie had mentioned her mom was visiting soon and staying with her instead of with Mia and Sean, but she had said nothing about Avery visiting this week or any other time in the near future. He wondered if Avery had made a special trip because she'd been unsuccessful at changing Angie's mind over the phone about the sequel to *A Prince to Call Her Own.* If she had flown across the country hoping a face-to-face would have better luck, he hoped she handled disappointment well. When they'd discussed it, Angie had been adamant that she had no interest in working on the sequel or any other project right now.

Sounds good. Are we still on for tomorrow?

He'd gotten two tickets from Jimmy for Tuesday's game between Boston and Baltimore. Angie planned to meet him at the office so they could grab a quick dinner before going to Fenway.

Yep, looking forward to it.
Me too.

With nothing left to keep him at work, Dakota powered off his computer and headed out. Later than he often left the office, he didn't hit any traffic on the way back to North Salem.

Most nights during the summer, he'd throw something on the grill when he got home. Unfortunately, he had nothing to grill in the house. For the most part, he went grocery shopping every two weeks and almost always on Sunday mornings. Yesterday he'd had much more enjoyable things to do than walking around the supermarket. With no leftovers in the refrigerator either, he had two options for dinner: either a peanut butter and jelly sandwich or one of the frozen meals he kept in the freezer for occasions like this.

After popping a chicken pot pie in the microwave, he retrieved his laptop from the living room. He used the device for email, paying bills, and checking a handful of news and sports sites. He never visited the websites associated with *The Star Insider* or *Today Magazine*, but he knew of them. And if the media had gotten a hold of the picture he'd seen tonight or one like it, those websites would have it posted.

He typed the words *Star Insider* into his favorite search engine. Immediately it brought up the website for the popular entertainment television show. The main picture on the page featured a musician he'd never heard of with a woman. The site didn't list the woman's name, and while she looked familiar, he couldn't recall who she was or whether she was an actress or a singer. Dakota scrolled through the next few stories. None of them mentioned Angie or displayed the picture of them together.

Closing out the site, he brought up the one for *Today Magazine*. The picture smack in the center of the page was of someone he recognized, but thankfully it wasn't Angie. Instead, it was a photo of Gage Larson and his wife, Maryann. Now a well-known musician, Gage and his wife grew up in North Salem and lived there until recently. Like he'd done on the other website, he scrolled through the various stories and pictures. When he again found nothing, he closed the laptop. While the picture still could be floating around, he took the fact that those two sites didn't have it as a good sign.

THANKS to a rolled-over tractor trailer on Interstate 93, Shane had been in traffic for almost two hours, so instead of the trip back to North Salem taking three hours, it had taken him almost five. On a different night, the extra-long drive home would've bothered him. Tonight he was too giddy for anything as minor as traffic to annoy him.

After leaving the log cabin-style home in Jefferson, they'd gone back to Cathy's office and prepared his offer on the property. He'd never bought a house before, but he knew it wasn't uncommon to offer less than the asking price with the understanding that the homeowners might come back with a counteroffer. Now that he'd found the perfect place, he didn't want to play around and risk losing out on the property. Rather than offer a lower dollar amount, he'd offered the full asking price.

He was at a rest stop getting gas and a soda when Cathy called and gave him the good news. The current owners accepted his offer. He'd already gone through the preapproval process at the bank, so unless something unexpected came up, the place would belong to him in about a month. Just a few more weeks and finally he and Angie could start their life together.

Should he stop by and tell her the good news tonight? Or would it be better to wait and surprise her? He'd never liked surprises, but some people did.

Shane turned down her street and parked a few houses away from hers. Angie's house was in complete darkness. Did that mean she was asleep or was she out? Her older sister

Mia lived nearby. He'd seen them walking together. She might have gone there to see Mia and her niece.

Headlights bounced off his rearview mirror, and Shane ducked lower in his seat before the car passed by. Instead of continuing down the road, it turned. At the same time, the exterior lights on Angie's house came on and the garage door went up. Inching up in his seat, he watched the car pull into the garage. It wasn't the same vehicle he'd seen Angie driving last week. Tonight there was also an SUV in the garage that hadn't been there before. The garage door closed before Angie got out of the car, depriving him of a glimpse of her.

He waited for the interior lights to go on and for her to pass by one of the windows. It never happened. Instead, a few moments later, light appeared in the top middle window where he assumed the hallway was. After about the amount of time it would take someone to walk down to a room, the light went out once again, leaving the house in darkness.

He'd come by again either between his deliveries or before he went to the restaurant tomorrow night. In the meantime, he'd go home and get some sleep. He had a full day ahead of him.

THIRTEEN

LEANING across the car Saturday morning, Angie kissed Dakota on the cheek. "I'll see you in a few hours." When he picked her up last night, she had suspected she'd end up spending the night at his house. But since he hadn't invited her beforehand, she hadn't packed even a toothbrush, let alone the dress she'd borrowed from Mia for the wedding today.

He waited in the driveway until she opened the front door and waved in his direction before backing into the street.

The smell of fresh flowers hit her the moment she stepped inside. The cause of the delightful scent sat in what she'd turned into a library. Yesterday after coming home from a walk with Mia and Natalie, she'd found an enormous arrangement of flowers on the front steps. The small card attached only read Welcome To Town. There was no name signed to the message, but judging by the handwriting, a woman had filled out the card. A call to the local florist who delivered the arrangement hadn't helped solve the mystery. The employee who answered the phone could only tell her the order was placed via their website early Thursday afternoon.

It wasn't the first time she received flowers or some other token from an anonymous fan. Before she left the spotlight, Mia had received them too. It simply came with the job. Rather than worry about it, she'd put the arrangement on an end table where she could enjoy it.

Angie was halfway up the front staircase when the doorbell rang. "Please don't let it be someone trying to sell me something or asking for my vote."

Wednesday afternoon a woman campaigning for Gina Hammond, one of the candidates running against Brett Sherbrooke for the open Senate seat, had stopped at the house. Not wanting to be rude, she'd stood there for at least half an hour as the woman explained why she was supporting Gina and urging Angie to vote for her as well. This morning she didn't have time to stand on the step while someone sang the praises of some politician. Especially since she'd decided which candidate she would vote for when she went to the polls.

She peeked out the window, but it wasn't another campaigner. A man dressed in a Door2Door Express delivery uniform stood there holding a package.

Over the past few days, she'd been busy shopping both on the internet and at various furniture and specialty stores. Much of what she'd purchased, especially on the internet, were gifts for Natalie, but she'd also ordered several things for the house too. Since she'd decided to only have the kitchen and bathrooms renovated, she'd hired a painter to come in and freshen up the rest of the home. He was starting next week. The additional furniture she'd ordered so far would arrive after he finished. She'd never painted, but common sense told her an empty room would be easier to work in. The numerous non-furniture items she'd purchased had been arriving for the past few days. Some she'd been home to receive, and others they had left on the front step.

Opening the door, Angie recognized Shane immediately.

"Good morning, Angie," he greeted. "I'm sorry to bother you, but this package requires a signature."

She accepted the box and the signature device. "Don't worry about it. I was already up, Shane."

"This is a gorgeous house. Are you all settled in?"

"Not even close. But I'm enjoying being in town." Angie handed him back the signature device and waited for him to leave.

He didn't. Instead, he nodded. "I moved back to North Salem a couple of years ago because I thought I missed it. Now I'm counting the days until I leave again. I'm buying a house up near the White Mountains."

Just because she liked North Salem didn't mean everyone did. "My sister told me it's beautiful up there." Hoping he'd get the hint and leave, she took a step back inside. "I hope it all goes smoothly for you. Have a nice day."

"You too." Shane smiled. Although she couldn't explain it, the sight sent a shiver through her body, and it took all her self-control not to slam the door in his face and lock it.

Whatever purchase was in the box didn't matter at the moment, so she left the unopened package near the foot of her bed before popping into the master bathroom and filling the tub.

Stepping into the warm water, the memory of Shane's smile surfaced, and she shivered despite the water's temperature. Exactly what about it made her uncomfortable, she had no idea. However, she hoped he didn't deliver any more of her packages to the house. And if he did, she hoped they were ones that didn't require a signature so he could leave them on the doorstep.

~

TO SOME DEGREE, the scene outside St. Mark's Church resembled the one there last fall on Mia and Sean's wedding day. Or more specifically, their second wedding day. Few people knew it, but her sister and her brother-in-law were already married the day Father Perkins performed their ceremony. Conscious of the media circus that would descend on North Salem, Mia and Sean had a small private ceremony on Martha's Vineyard weeks earlier. Actually, it'd been so private that only five people—Mia's friends who owned the house; Tony Bates, Sean's best friend; Tony's wife, Cat; and Avery—had witnessed it. Mia had invited her too, but unfortunately at the time, she'd been out of the country working on a movie, making it impossible for her to go.

Other than Avery and Mia, Angie hadn't told anyone she'd be here today. And while she kept somewhat active on her social media sites, she had mentioned nothing about her current move to North Salem. Had Avery let the fact that she'd be here today slip to some media outlet? It still annoyed Avery that she wouldn't accept any new projects. Her sister was even more upset that she'd decided to stay out of the spotlight altogether. Maybe Avery had let *Today Magazine* or one of the local news outlets know she'd be here today as a way to get Angie's name in the headlines. If the circus out there was Avery's fault, she was going to get an earful the next time they spoke.

Dakota snagged the last open spot in the church parking lot. "Striker hoped Maryann and Gage wouldn't be able to come today because he worried something like this would happen if they did."

Now the media gathered outside the church made sense. Gage Larson was the front man for the band Larson Pike. She'd met both him and his wife at Sean and Mia's wedding. In fact, the band had performed the music for the reception.

"Maryann and Ella have been friends for a long time, so

he couldn't ask her not to invite them. But he didn't want a scene like the one when your sister got married either. I'm sure it doesn't help that Drew and Kelsey are here too."

This time when he mentioned Drew McKenzie, she kept her mouth shut. "Hopefully the reporters and photographers don't ruin their day." She was used to the paparazzi being around, but even she'd be pissed if their presences somehow ruined her wedding day.

With the crowd on the lookout for Gage and his wife, they made it from the parking lot to the lawn without drawing any attention. Unfortunately, a photographer turned just as they were approaching the concrete walkway leading up to the church steps. Without so much as a hello first, he raised his camera and snapped a picture, then called out her name. The moment he spoke, all the reporters and cameras swung in her direction.

"Angelina, is it true you'll be staring in the sequel to *A Prince to Call Her Own* along with Chad DeMelo?" one reporter with a cameraman behind her called out.

"Ms. Tioy, are you a friend of the bride or the groom?" Marcy Blake, a reporter she'd spoken to in the past from *Today Magazine*, asked.

A third individual approached her with a cameraman in tow. Much like the reporter from *Today Magazine*, Angie recognized this one because she'd had previous dealings with her. Aimee Trainor was the host of *The Star Insider*, a popular entertainment talk show, and Angie could recall at least two interviews she'd done with her.

Unless Angie and Dakota made a run for it, there was no way they could get inside the church before Aimee reached them. That was of course assuming the woman didn't follow them inside. From the dealings she'd had with Aimee in the past as well as the dealing her friends had had, Angie wouldn't put it past the television show host to follow them into St. Mark's if it meant getting a good story before everyone else.

"Sorry about this," Angie whispered before Aimee and her cameraman reached them.

Dakota didn't reply. Instead, he squeezed her hand and remained by her side.

Aimee smiled, showing off two rows of incredibly white teeth. They were so white they appeared fake against her bronzed skin. "I covered your sister's wedding here last year. I didn't know you had ties to the town as well. Considering all the people who have connections to North Salem, it must be a very special place."

Yep, she remembered seeing Aimee lurking around outside the church last fall, along with at least half a dozen other reporters. "You're right, it is a special place." Telling Aimee Trainor she lived in North Salem was tantamount to telling the entire world, so if the television host ever found out she lived here, it wouldn't be because she mentioned it.

Aimee turned her gaze and her bright white smile in Dakota's direction and gave him a not-so-subtle once-over before extending her hand. "I should've introduced myself sooner. Aimee Trainor. You may have seen me on *The Star Insider*."

"It's nice to meet you." Dakota's tone remained flat as he accepted Aimee's hand.

"Do you live in North Salem, Mister...?"

"Smith. I live nearby."

If Aimee planned to dig into Dakota's background and learn all she could, it would take a little more effort with only a last name—especially with a last name as common as Smith. Angie guessed it was precisely why Dakota had only given her that much.

Perhaps aware she'd get no additional information from Dakota, she turned her attention back to Angie. "In June there were reports that things were heating up between you and Devon Cash on the set in Rome. Since you're here today with Mr. Smith, I assume you've ended your relationship with Devon."

"Devon and I are friends and coworkers. That's all we've ever been."

In reality they weren't even friends. She couldn't stand the guy, but she'd never tell someone like Aimee Trainor that. When they got a moment alone, though, she would explain her true feelings to Dakota. Considering Aimee's comment, she had to.

"If you'll please excuse us, we need to get inside." She had no idea when the bride would arrive, but she didn't want to be outside causing a scene when Ella did.

Aimee flashed another blinding smile and waved her hand. "Of course. I understand. Thank you so much for your time this afternoon, Angelina."

Before anyone else moved into the space the host vacated, they started walking again. This time they made it to the top of the church steps.

"Gage," someone in the crowd called.

Angie stopped long enough to glance back and see Gage Larson and his wife approach the edge of the grass. En masse, the reporters surged toward the popular musician.

"Maybe the church should look into installing a secret underground entrance." Dakota pulled open the door and waited for her to precede him into the building.

"I think you're right."

NEITHER HE NOR Angie had found the picture Jared showed him on any media site. Since no one else Dakota knew mentioned it to him, he assumed that whoever had taken the picture at the block party hadn't shared it with too many people. The photographs of them together taken moments ago would be a whole different story. He hadn't recognized any of the reporters outside, but he had recognized the name of the Boston-based news outlet printed on the side of a van and the popular entertainment show. Unlike the Boston-based news channel, which covered actual local and international stories as well as the weather, *The Star Insider* was all about entertaining people regardless of how factual the stories were. So whether or not he liked it, soon his face would be all over the internet as well as on the popular entertainment show. And it was anyone's guess what kind of story the reporters would concoct to go along with the photos.

"I'm really sorry about that." Angie tilted her head toward his, and if they were anywhere other than a church, he'd turn and kiss her.

He'd been half expecting their relationship to become public knowledge since the evening the woman on the ghost tour recognized Angie. Once Jared showed him the picture, he'd known it was simply a matter of time.

"It's not your fault they're here. They camped outside because they got wind of the fact that Gage was coming."

Angie crossed her legs, allowing the slit up the side of the dress to widen. The sight of the bare skin brought back the memory of her legs wrapped around his waist this morning in bed. Despite his current location, his body reacted to the memory. Bad idea or not, he couldn't stop himself from placing his hand on the exposed skin.

She glanced over her shoulder at the main doors into the building. "I really hope none of them try to follow Gage and Maryann inside the church."

Not a single reporter had made it inside the day Sean and Mia got married, but they'd also hired security guards to make sure none of them passed through the doors. Ella and

Striker didn't have guards waiting to stop anyone who didn't belong from entering the church.

"You and me both."

Angie covered his hand with hers, something she often did when they were sitting together regardless of whether they were alone or out in public. And he enjoyed it far more than he'd thought possible.

"Tomorrow Mia invited us over for a cookout. Avery will be there, but she won't stay long. She has plans to meet our cousin Rae Ann in Boston. And Sean's sister Taylor will be over. Tony and Cat are planning to go, and a few of Sean's other friends might stop by too. I told Mia I wasn't sure what we were doing and I'd get back to her."

Avery had been in town all week, but he hadn't seen her. Angie hadn't spent a lot of time with her either, and not because Avery hadn't invited her along on her various day trips. Angie hadn't gone into specific details, but she'd mentioned that Monday night Avery had once again given her a hard time about her decision to make some career changes. Until Avery was willing to at least keep her opinion to herself, Angie didn't want to have any extended visits with her sister, which was why she'd turned down all of Avery's invitations.

"What do you want to do?" It wasn't uncommon for him to spend long periods of time with people he didn't want to be around. It kind of went with the job. Judging by what Angie had shared, he feared Avery would be one of those people. But he liked Sean and Mia, and more importantly, he cared about Angie and enjoyed making her happy.

Her fingertips moved up his fingers before making tiny circles on his hand. Much like the sight of the bare skin, the caress transported his mind back to their time in bed this morning. She'd done something similar with her fingers on his chest after they'd made love.

"I want to go. It's been over forty-eight hours since I saw Natalie. And I haven't seen Sean's sister since the spring, and I like Taylor." Angie stopped her caress and laced her fingers with his. "I don't think Avery will say anything with you and Taylor there."

There was a slight change in the noise inside the church, and Dakota looked back toward the door where the cause stood. Everyone seemed to have their eyes fixed on Gage and Maryann as they walked down the center aisle. Gage appeared unaffected by all the attention, but there was no missing the blush on Maryann's cheeks. He waited to see if any of the reporters from outside followed the couple inside, but the door remained closed. Once the well-known musician and his wife sat, the noise in the church shifted again as guests went back to their previous conversations while they waited for the ceremony to begin.

"Looks like the reporters are staying outside." He tried adjusting his position, but it didn't help. The wooden pews were not designed with comfort in mind.

"I'll reserve judgment until the ceremony starts. They might be waiting out there hoping to get a picture and a statement from Mia."

He hadn't seen Mia and Sean so far, but he knew they were coming.

"When I see Mia, I'll let her know we'll be over tomorrow."

Dakota was again in the process of trying to get a little more comfortable when Striker and his best man, Mack, joined Father Perkins at the altar.

"I'm surprised Mack is here," Angie whispered. "Didn't Jessie only come home from the hospital a few days ago?"

Mack had taken this week off as well as next so he could be home with his wife and family. And if the wedding was for anyone other than Striker, Dakota knew his friend would be at home right now helping Jessie take care of the twins and Grace. But Striker and Mack had been close friends since elementary school, and Mack never let his friends down.

"Mack's sister is over at the house in case Jessie needs any help. And Mack told me he's only staying at the reception long enough to give the best man speech and see them cut the cake." If he had a newborn baby at home, he wouldn't want to be away any longer than necessary either.

Until now the sound of quiet conversations had filled the church, but with Striker and the priest waiting, Joyce, the pianist, started playing. On cue, the doors into the church's main foyer opened, and an adorable vision in white came down the aisle accompanied by a young boy dressed in a tuxedo matching Striker's and Mack's. As if she'd done it a million times, Kerry, Ella's niece and flower girl, smiled as she slowly made her way to the altar. The ring bearer didn't share Kerry's smiles. Instead, he looked about ready to cry. Still, he successfully reached Striker and Mack without breaking into tears or running off in search of his parents. Cat and Tony came next, followed by Kelsey on the arm of a man he didn't know. Striker and the man resembled each other, though, and since his friend didn't have any brothers, Dakota pegged the guy with Kelsey as Striker's cousin.

Once Claire, Ella's older sister and maid of honor, reached the rest of the wedding party, the music changed and the guests stood. Moments later Ella and her father started down the aisle.

Whenever he saw Ella, she appeared happy. Today the word happy didn't do justice to the way she looked. Dakota glanced back at Striker. The man's expression mirrored Ella's. The previous year the couple had hit a rough patch in their relationship, but everyone here today could see how in love they were.

Relationships weren't easy. He knew it firsthand. He'd

once thought he'd found the woman he would spend the rest of his life with. When Sherrilyn called off their engagement four months before the wedding, it had been like a knife through the chest. It wasn't until several months later that he'd recognized all the signs suggesting they weren't right for each other. Regardless of his failed engagement, one of these days he wanted what his parents and Mack had and Striker was about to have. It was way too early to know if this new relationship with Angie would ever get that far, but he wanted to find out.

FOURTEEN

"I'd never tell Mia this because her wedding was beautiful, but it was too big. I think she had something like three hundred guests at the reception."

He didn't know how many guests Ella and Striker expected tonight, but even though this was the largest ballroom at the Hawthorne Hotel, there was no way it could comfortably hold that many people. The room at the Harbor House where Mia and Sean had their reception had been at least twice as large as this one.

Angie reached for her glass of wine but didn't pick it up. "I'd rather have something more like this, or maybe even the private ceremony my sister had on Martha's Vineyard."

It wasn't any of his business, but he couldn't let the comment go either. "What private ceremony?"

She scooted her chair closer and leaned in. "Mia and Sean got married on Martha's Vineyard a few weeks before the ceremony at St. Mark's because they didn't want the media spoiling the day."

Considering the scene he remembered from their wedding

day and the one outside the church today, he couldn't say he blamed the couple. "I don't blame them. I wouldn't want the craziness that surrounded them then either."

They hadn't discussed their plans for after the reception yet. He assumed she'd be spending the night with him again. More than once, though, he'd assumed something and had it come back to bite him in the ass, so he tried to avoid it. "You're welcome to stay with me tonight. We can stop at your place and get your clothes after this. But if you want me to just drop you off after the reception, I will."

She slipped her free hand under the table and ran it across his thigh, not stopping until she reached the junction between leg and torso. "I've been looking forward to a late-night swim all day." Angie moved her hand to the right and settled over his zipper. Whatever blood was pumping through his brain made a swift detour south.

"But let's make a quick stop at my house when we get back so I can grab some clothes. Then we can head straight to my sister's house tomorrow afternoon." She kissed his cheek before using her other hand to lift her wineglass to her lips.

If she planned on torturing him tonight, he was going to give it right back to her. Like she'd done, Dakota moved his hand under the table and flicked the dress's split apart. The move earned him a sideways look from Angie, but she gave no indication he should put his hands back on the table. Slowly he traced a path up her inner thigh. He'd almost reached his final destination when Mia and Sean arrived at the table.

"Did Daniella Nault stop you outside too?" Mia sat down in the chair Sean pulled out for her.

Under the table, Angie patted his hand. "No, we must have gotten inside before she arrived." She clasped both hands on the table in front of her. "Was she at the church? I didn't see her."

The fact that he had no idea who they were talking about must have been evident on his face, because rather than answer her sister, Mia said, "Daniella Nault is a reporter for *The Star Report* magazine."

When they'd entered the hotel, there hadn't been any media outside yet.

"I don't think she was at St. Mark's, but I wasn't really looking for her either. When we spotted all the people waiting for Gage out front, we used the back door to get in the church."

"And you didn't think to share that the church has a back door?"

Mia shrugged. "Sorry, it didn't occur to me to tell you. So are you coming by tomorrow?" Before Angie could answer, she held up a hand. "Before you say yes or no, Avery's plans changed. She isn't meeting Rae Ann in Boston."

Angie and Mia exchanged a look he couldn't read but left no doubt in his mind the two sisters were communicating some tidbit of knowledge they didn't want to share with either him or Sean.

"We're coming. What time should we get there?"

Sometime between the maid of honor's speech and the best man's speech, Angie slipped her hand under the table and settled it on his thigh again. It remained there throughout much of dinner. When she and Mia had left the table a moment ago, she'd finally moved it. Without her hand there, he felt somehow incomplete and lonely. And considering he sat in a room filled with people and Sean was across the table from him, he shouldn't feel lonely.

"I hope you're ready for more craziness like what was outside the church this morning," Sean said from across the table. "Now that the media knows Angie is involved with someone, they're going to try to learn everything they can about you."

Dakota stopped searching for Angie and focused his attention on Sean. "Yeah, I had a similar thought while we were inside the church. Any suggestions for dealing with the reporters?"

Although the media didn't bother Mia as much on a daily basis anymore, they'd printed more than one story featuring pictures of her and Sean.

"Say as little as possible."

That he could do.

"With Angie taking a break from acting, the media will eventually lose interest in her. At least that's how it was for Mia. Yeah, they still bug her occasionally, but nothing like when we first met. And from the sound of it, Angie plans on sticking around here and writing. Between you and me, I never pictured her as a writer, but Mia says Angie's been doing it since she was young."

"Hey, I know how to knit and sew. We all have hidden talents."

"You can knit?" Angie placed a glass of wine in front of him before she took her seat. "Gram tried showing me when I was about seven or eight, but I couldn't get the hang of it."

She took a sip of her drink, and when she pulled the glass away, a droplet of wine remained on her bottom lip. If they were alone, he'd lean closer and lick the liquid off. Unfortunately, this was not the time or place.

"Maybe you can try teaching me." Picking up her fork, she closed her mouth around a bite of cake, and Dakota could do nothing but stare as the memory of where those lips had been this morning materialized. Much like earlier in the evening, his body reacted, and he wondered if anyone other than Mia and Sean would say anything if they left now.

Dakota dropped his eyes to his watch and then reached for his ice water. Not that he expected a cold drink to help cool him down.

"Hey, if I have to dance at least once before we go, you do too." Sean's comment had Dakota looking his way. Sean's smile told him the guy had a damn good idea of what was going through his head.

"It's a wedding, not a funeral. We need to dance." Mia grabbed Sean's hand and stood up. "C'mon, I love this song."

With reluctance, Sean came to his feet. His friend hated dancing. Even at his own wedding reception, he'd done as little of it as possible.

"If you're not here when we get back, see you both tomorrow." With her final comment, Mia led Sean toward the dance floor.

Dakota watched Sean wrap his arms around his wife and pull her close. When Mia whispered something into his ear, Sean nodded before kissing her.

"Do you want to dance?" Mia was right, this was a wedding, and people usually danced at weddings.

Angie put her fork down next to the plate and took one more sip of her wine. "Sure."

After finding an open spot, Angie put her arms around his neck and pressed her body against his. Despite the layers of clothes between them, his skin tingled wherever they touched, and his body was aware of every breath she took in. Although at least one hundred people surrounded them, it was like none of them existed. It was just the two of them moving as one to the music.

WHEN HER CELL phone on the end table chirped, Angie considered ignoring it. Dakota was in the kitchen talking to a coworker, and since she'd seen Mia less than two hours ago, she doubted her sister would send her a message now.

If the message was from Mom, she'd rather deal with her

later. The last few times they'd talked hadn't been pleasant conversations. In fact, she was already dreading Mom's visit in October, and it was still several weeks away.

The device chirped a second time, which meant she'd received a second message. Picking up the phone, she read the first text from Avery and then clicked on the link in the second one.

She groaned when the website for *The Star Insider* opened. Even worse, right below a picture of Gage and his wife arriving at the church, there was a picture of her and Dakota. Scrolling down, she passed the video uploaded to the site as well and scanned the story instead. Before she finished reading it, a third message from Avery popped up.

Nice job, sis. You're also on Today Magazine's website and Boston's Channel Five's website. I guess going to the wedding today was a good idea.

Her sister might think so, since it kept Angie in the public eye. She didn't. Earlier Dakota had appeared unbothered by the cameras and reporters. Once he saw his face on the internet, he might have second thoughts about being with her. Not everyone liked being the center of attention. Her brother-in-law hated it. No one had been happier than him when the media stopped following Mia's every move.

Thanks for letting me know. See you tomorrow.

Now was not the time to remind Avery she'd made up her mind and didn't plan on returning to Los Angeles.

She was scrolling through the pictures on *Today Magazine's* website when Dakota returned.

"Sorry about that." He dropped back on the sofa and reached for the remote control.

"Everything okay?" Dakota rarely received calls when they were together, so if a coworker called on a Saturday night, it could be about something serious.

"Yeah, Jared wanted to tell me his daughter saw our

picture on that entertainment show's website. There are some making the rounds on different social media sites too."

Well, at least she didn't need to break the bad news to him. "I know. Avery sent me the links. *Today Magazine* has some up, and so does Channel Five News." She passed him her cell phone. "Take a look."

Without turning the baseball game back on, he put the remote down and scrolled through the pictures in silence. Like on the other media sites, pictures of Gage and his wife as well as Drew and Kelsey joined theirs.

She wanted to ask him how he felt about the situation. Instead, she bit down on the inside of her cheek and watched his face for any hint as to what was going through his head. Unfortunately, his expression gave nothing away.

An eternity passed before he handed the device back to her. "I hope the camera guy from the entertainment show got my good side. The photos on this site are crap. I could take a picture of the two of us together myself and it'd look better than what the photographer took."

Unprepared for his comment, she laughed, releasing at least some of her nervousness. Before bringing up the other website, she glanced at the screen again. "I think they're pretty good." She handed the phone back to him so he could see what *The Star Insider* had published. "Are you okay with this?" If she heard the nervous wobble in her voice, he had too.

Much like with the first site, he scrolled through the various pictures. "I'm not thrilled about it, but I expected it would happen eventually."

Relief seeped through every inch of her body. "They'll get bored with us quickly." Unless an individual was regularly doing things to catch the media's attention, reporters moved on to more interesting stories.

"Until they do, Jared and a few others at work are going

to give me hell every day. Not that I blame them. I'd do the same to them if the tables were reversed."

When he handed her back the phone, the website for *The Star Insider* was still open. She hadn't thought about the comment Aimee made outside the church since they left the reporter behind. Aimee Trainor's smiling face brought it back.

"There was talk in June that Devon Cash and I were together. We weren't. At the church, I told Aimee we're friends, but honestly, I can't stand Devon. I've never worked with a man with a bigger ego. If his head gets much bigger, no one will be able to stand in the same room as him."

"No need to explain. When you told the reporter the two of you were never involved, I believed you." He reached for the remote control again. "Do you want to finish the game now or go for a swim and watch it after?"

The baseball game had been on while they were at the reception, and he'd recorded it so they could watch it later. When his friend called, the fourth inning had been about to start. "Let's finish the game first. I have something else in mind for after our swim."

EXCEPT TO CHECK THE WEATHER, Shane didn't bother with the local news station. If he wanted to know what was going on, regardless of whether it was in the state or on the other side of the country, he could find the information on the internet. When he did go in search of news, he saw no need to visit any of the popular entertainment sites. Whether an actress in Beverly Hills was sleeping with the husband of a popular musician didn't change his life.

Once his break started and he went into the employee

break room, those were the exact sites he planned to check out.

Shane looked at his watch. When he worked Saturday nights at Masterson's, his shifts never dragged. The restaurant was too busy on the weekends for it to happen. But ever since he'd overheard two customers talking about the pictures they'd seen of Angelina Troy and her handsome date on the evening news, time had slowed to a snail's pace.

They might be wrong. He delivered the desserts to table eight and left their receipt. When they requested nothing further, he walked back to the kitchen to grab his own dinner order.

Only Mara, the restaurant owner's granddaughter, was in the employee break room when he entered. She stood in front of her locker mirror reapplying her makeup.

"Hey, Shane." She glanced back at him before closing her locker door. "Is it still busy out there?"

He set his plate down on the table and crossed to his locker. "Not a single empty table."

Mara slipped the combination lock back in place. "Enjoy your dinner. See you in a bit."

He waited until the door closed behind Mara, then pulled his cell phone from his locker. Maybe if he tried hard enough, the name of a popular media site would come to him, but he didn't have a lot of time or patience. After pressing the internet icon, he typed Angelina Troy into the search engine. Seconds later, a list of websites appeared. He skipped the biography site at the top of the list and pressed the link for *The Star Insider*. It sounded like the type of site that would have the information he was looking for.

The top pictures were of Gage Larson, a guy Shane went to school with until ninth grade, and his wife, Maryann. They'd played on the same town soccer team in elementary and middle school and had often gotten into arguments both on and off the field.

Shane scrolled down past the short article under Gage's pictures. He stopped when the next set of photos appeared. Angie stared back at him, but she wasn't alone. A man he'd seen in the restaurant several times stood next to her. He couldn't tell if the guy had his arm around Angie or not, but they were standing close. Rage raced through him, and he raised his arm to throw the device across the room. Common sense jabbed him before he released the phone.

Lowering his hand, he looked back at the screen. Then, unlike with the other short article, he read the sentences under the photos of Angie.

Angelina Troy, the star of the fall blockbuster A Prince to Call Her Own, *arrived at St. Mark's Church in North Salem this morning with her new boyfriend. St. Mark's Church is also where Mia Troy, Angelina's older sister, married North Salem native Sean O'Brien last year. Many of you may also remember North Salem is the very town where legendary playboy Jake Sherbrooke met his wife a few years ago. With so many finding love in town, I can't help but wonder if we'll soon be returning to report on Angelina and Mr. Smith's wedding.*

Shane scrolled back up to the first picture. His Angie looked beautiful, but she always did. Even this morning when he delivered her package and it was obvious she hadn't combed her hair or put on any makeup, she looked gorgeous.

He moved the phone closer. She wasn't smiling in all the photos, but in the center one she was.

She wants me to see these pictures. It all made sense now. Angie was trying to make him jealous because it was taking him so long. She'd gone out in public with another man to send him a message. Angie wasn't dating Smith. She was using him.

The rest of his anger drained away and he closed the website. *Don't worry, Angie. Just a few more weeks and we'll never be apart again. I promise.*

FIFTEEN

ANGIE GLANCED at the motorcycle and then at him.

"If you'd rather use the car, it's okay."

It wasn't uncommon for Dakota to just get on his Harley and ride for hours with no destination in mind on the weekends. He wanted to take Angie along, but he wanted her to enjoy the rides as much as he did. But he knew motorcycles weren't for everyone. His ex-fiancée had hated his bike. Not once when they'd been together had she been willing to even try a short trip on it. Last night Angie had agreed immediately when he suggested taking it to Sean and Mia's house this afternoon, but now it was obvious she was having second and third thoughts about it. He didn't want her doing anything she wasn't comfortable with.

After taking in a deep breath, she accepted the helmet he held toward her. "Mia and Sean's house is only four or five miles from here. So if I really hate it, the ride won't be a long one."

"Are you sure?"

"Positive."

Before she put her helmet on and made it difficult to kiss

her, he pulled her in close and brushed his lips across hers. "I think you're going to love it. And if you don't, when it's time to leave tonight, I'll drive back here and get my car."

He released her and took a step away. If they remained this close for too long, he'd suggest they head back inside and stay there for the rest of the day rather than enjoy a friendly cookout.

"It made Mia nervous the first few times she went on Sean's motorcycle, but now she loves it. She says it's a unique experience. I'm sure I'll be fine before we even reach the end of the street."

Dakota waited for Angie to get settled behind him before reaching for his helmet hanging from the handlebars. "All set?"

Her arms came around his waist, and she leaned into his back. "Ready."

A nervous edge remained in her voice, but he didn't question her decision again. After securing his helmet, he started the engine.

When he passed Brett's house, the same dark green Mustang convertible he'd seen there several times now was in the driveway. At the house next door, Mack and Grace were shooting hoops in the adjustable basketball net he'd recently set up. Even Mrs. Mitchell was in her front yard gardening.

He kept his speed well below the limit as they continued toward the stop sign at the end of the street. Although Angie didn't say anything, he noticed she loosened the viselike grip she'd originally had around his waist.

He took that as a good sign.

When he turned on Fender Drive, he increased his speed and waited for her grip to tighten again. It didn't.

Dakota only recognized one of the three vehicles in the driveway as he pulled in behind Tony's truck. Once he turned off the engine, Angie's arms moved from around his waist, and she pulled away. Immediately, he missed having her pressed against him.

"What did you think?" He accepted the helmet she held toward him and hung it from the handlebars.

The ride might have been one of the shortest he'd taken in a long time, but he'd enjoyed every moment of it. Until today, he'd never had a girlfriend ride behind him, so he'd never realized how much more enjoyable a ride could be with a woman you cared about pressed against you and her arms around your waist.

"Loved it. Mia was right. It's unlike anything else I've done." She slipped off the bike and held out her hand. "Next time we need to go for a longer ride."

"If it's nice next weekend, we can take a ride along the Kancamagus Highway." He hadn't been up that way all summer.

"Talk about a mouthful. I've never heard of it. Where is it?"

"The northern part of New Hampshire. It stretches for about thirty-four miles or so. It goes straight through the White Mountain National Forest. And there are some great spots along it for hiking. Or we can ride out to the Castle in the Clouds." He'd wanted to check out the mansion since he'd learned of it.

"I'll leave it up to you."

Mia and Max greeted them at the door. "Everyone's outside." She hugged first Angie and then him. He'd discovered the first time Sean introduced him to Mia that she was a hugger. It didn't matter if it'd been two days since she last saw you or two months, a hug was part of her greeting when you walked in her house.

None of his family members were huggers, including him. He much preferred a hello or perhaps a handshake. Regardless, he returned Mia's hug.

"Go ahead out. I need to go upstairs and get Natalie; she just woke up from her nap. I'll be there in a minute." Mia started for the stairs.

"I'll go get her," Angie offered before her sister's foot touched the first step.

"She probably needs a change."

"Don't worry about it," she replied before looking at him. "I'll meet you outside."

Taylor, Sean's much younger half sister, noticed him first when he walked onto the back deck. "Hey, Dakota."

The greeting caused the dark-haired woman sitting on the chair across from Taylor to look his way. He'd never met Avery. She'd flown in the day before Sean and Mia's wedding and then home to California the next day. If she'd visited since then, he'd never seen her around.

While Angie and Mia shared a strong family resemblance to the point that some might confuse them, the only similarity between Avery and her sisters was her hair color.

Sean left his spot near the grill and clapped him on the back. "Glad you guys made it. I don't think you've met Mia and Angie's sister, Avery." He inclined his head in Avery's direction.

Unlike Mia, Avery didn't get up to give him a hug as part of her greeting. Instead, she gave him an odd little smile. "It's nice to finally meet you. Everyone is going crazy trying to learn more about you. I've received calls from three different magazines this morning. And Skylar, Angie's agent, has gotten a few too."

He held back a groan. Yesterday, he'd intentionally only given the reporter a last name. From the little Angie shared about her sister, he didn't think she'd be as discreet if someone asked for more information regarding who he was.

"Don't be surprised if a few show up at your door in the

next week or so. Once they get to the bottom of who you are, they're going to want to know all there is about you."

His first instinct was to ask Avery just what she'd told the individuals who'd called her. Dakota kept the question in his head. Maybe later he'd ask Angie to talk to her sister instead.

"Let's hope they don't, because they'll get a demand to leave the property. And if they refuse, the police will be by to show them off." The occasional political campaigner or salesman he would tolerate. If even a single reporter showed up, he'd send them packing without so much as a polite hello first. If they refused, he had no qualms about calling the local police to report a trespasser.

"Consider getting a big dog," Sean suggested. "A lot of reporters used to take one look at Max and get right back into their cars."

Dakota looked over at Max, who was sitting near Taylor getting the fur behind his ears scratched. The dog was huge, but he'd never even heard Max bark. The odds of the dog hurting anyone seemed slim to none. Still, he understood how some might see Max and not stick around to find out if he was friendly or not.

Avery gave her brother-in-law a dirty look. "Answer their questions and they'll go away too. The world loves Angie. She's one of the hottest actresses around right now. People want to know everything about her. If you're going to spend time with her while she's in town, you need to accept that."

He had a great comeback prepared. Unfortunately, he didn't get a chance to release it, because Angie stepped outside. The sight of her cradling Natalie in her arms while speaking softly to her robbed him of the ability to form words.

Whether or not to have children had been one of the many things he and Sherrilyn had disagreed about. Dakota wanted them someday, and she didn't. She believed they would get in the way of her career. These days he didn't think too much about children. Seeing Angie standing there with her niece brought to mind all the reasons he wanted to be a father someday. And based on the way she went on about her niece, Angie would make a wonderful mother.

"How's the house coming?" Steve's question forced him to look away from Angie and Natalie and use his brain again.

One of Sean and Tony's friends, he'd gotten to know Steve a little since he occasionally attended their monthly poker games. Last he'd heard, Steve was single again. Considering the looks he kept sending Avery's way, he would love to change his relationship status. Dakota didn't think Steve had a chance in hell with Avery though. From the little Angie had told him about her sister, Avery wasn't the type to get involved with an average Joe from a small town.

"Good. I just want to paint the upstairs bathroom and everything will be done."

CRAP. Angie heard the tail end of her sister's comment and made a beeline for Dakota. She hadn't caught the beginning of their conversation, but she had a sinking sensation the media had reached out to Avery hoping to get more information about Dakota. She assumed Avery's suggestion about "accepting it" referred to accepting that photos of them would appear in various places.

Angie greeted the other guests before turning her attention Avery's way. "Hey, Avery." She took the seat closest to her sister. If she sat between Avery and Dakota, perhaps her sister wouldn't talk to him much. "Is Rae Ann sick? Mia said you were meeting her in Boston today."

Avery shook her head. "Karen is. Rae Ann didn't want to leave her with Aunt Nicole, and Eric is traveling for work. Next time I'm out this way, we can get together."

Considering how infrequently Avery came to the East Coast, it might be a long time before the two went out. "When are you leaving?" Avery's visits were always short. Angie doubted this one would last much longer.

"Not sure." Avery shrugged, then moved her sunglasses onto her head as a cloud passed overhead, momentarily blocking the sun's glare. "Before you came out, I was telling Dakota that Marcy Blake, Daniella Nault, and a few others have reached out wanting to know the details about your relationship. You know, the usual stuff. Skylar has received similar calls."

"What did you tell them?" Angie mentally kicked herself. Last night when Avery sent her the links to the pictures, she should've asked her sister not to share any information. Although Avery didn't know a lot about Dakota, she did know his full name and where he lived. With those two pieces of information, the media could easily uncover more.

"The truth."

Since she held Natalie, clenching her fists was impossible. Instead, she ground her teeth together. Avery might be her sister and her former personal assistant, but she didn't have the right to share anything about her and Dakota's relationship with anyone. Especially since Angie intended to put acting behind her for the foreseeable future. More importantly, because Dakota wasn't used to finding his name and face plastered across every tabloid magazine and website around.

"Could you be a little more specific?"

Dakota touched her thigh as if he was telling her to not worry about it. She appreciated the gesture, but it didn't help diffuse her growing annoyance.

The cloud moved, once again putting Avery in the direct path of the sunlight, and she moved her sunglasses back into place. "I explained you and Dakota met in North Salem and that you'd been seeing each other a couple of weeks. Angie, we both know they could've asked anyone in town and gotten the same information."

Yeah, but at least then it wouldn't have come directly from her sister.

"It's not the end of the world," Dakota whispered in her ear.

When he'd brushed off the pictures last night, she'd been not only relieved but also touched. Their relationship was still new. There was nothing binding them together. He could've escorted her to the front door because he didn't want the craziness being with her might produce. Dakota's continued understanding now, especially since it had been Avery who gave the reporters his name and other details, endeared him even further to her. Already she suspected she was close to being in love with him. If he kept being as understanding and kind as he'd been so far, it'd be a done deal.

FOR THE FIRST time since she arrived, Angie was alone with both her sisters. Before they joined everyone outside again, Angie wanted to clarify a few things with Avery. "If Marcy Blake or anyone else calls you, don't under any circumstances share anything with them."

"Why? The more they print about you the better. We don't want the public and your fans to forget about you. Trust me, when you're ready to leave North Salem behind, you'll thank me."

Angie accepted the pastry box Mia handed her and considered placing the fresh fruit tart inside on her sister's face rather than the serving plate Mia set out. "Dakota's not like Anderson or Chad. He doesn't want his private life on public display. And for the thousandth time, I don't plan on leaving. I'll come back to LA to visit, but I have no intention of living there again."

"Everyone loves a chance in the spotlight. Dakota's no different. If he really was, he wouldn't have gotten involved with you." Once again, Avery used her "I'm older and I know everything" voice.

Angie disagreed. Yes, a lot of people would love a chance for fifteen minutes of fame, but not everyone. Angie had no doubts about which category Dakota fit into. "Think what you want, Avery. I'm not going to argue with you. But please refrain from answering any more questions. If we want to share details with the world, we will."

Avery's lips parted as if about to speak, but then she clamped them shut again and stared at her. "You're serious about staying here, aren't you?"

Hadn't she been telling Avery she intended to stay for weeks?

"I guess in the long run it doesn't matter where you live. Chad spends a lot of his time in Montana, and his career is as strong as ever. Nikki lives about half the year in Hawaii, and she has no shortage of work coming her way."

Wow, her sister was dense. Was it worth rehashing the same conversation they'd been having? Before Angie decided either way, Mia held a plate of cookies toward Avery.

"Can you bring these outside for me? I think Angie and I can manage the rest." Mia glanced in her direction and gave a subtle nod.

Neither of them spoke until Avery exited through the door.

"Ignore her. Avery doesn't understand. She did the same to me for months. Eventually, she'll give up." Mia leaned back against the counter and reached for the raspberry iced tea she'd poured.

"I've been trying to, but she's driving me batty. Every

time I talk to Avery, she mentions moving back." Although it might be impolite to start eating dessert before everyone else, she snagged a brownie off the plate near Mia's arm. "Did you make these?"

"I helped, but Taylor did most of the work when she got here this morning." Mia followed suit and grabbed a brownie as well. "Don't worry too much about Dakota. He didn't seem upset when Avery mentioned the media contacted her. He's an intelligent man. He knew being with you meant the media would get involved. And the Marcy Blakes of the world will get bored with the two of you just like they got bored with me and Sean."

She recognized everything Mia said as being the truth. Still, she'd prefer if their relationship stayed out of the media.

Mia leaned closer and dropped her voice even though they were alone in the kitchen. "I think Dakota loves you."

A shock wave raced through her body and left her insides vibrating in its wake. "I don't think he's there yet." Just because she might be a few baby steps from being in love with him didn't mean he'd reached the same point.

"You didn't see the way Dakota looked at you when you came outside from getting Natalie. But I did. He might have a great poker face when we play, but this afternoon it deserted him."

"Are you talking about Dakota?" Cat asked, entering the kitchen from the hallway.

Mia looked toward her friend. "Are you okay? Is there anything I can get for you? You look a little pale."

Several times since she and Dakota arrived, she'd seen Cat leave the group and go inside. The most recent time, she sprinted off the deck and into the house.

Cat poured herself a glass of the chilled herbal tea and took a slow sip. "I'm fine, but if you have some saltines, it would be great. They're the only things that seem to help settle my stomach." She sat down at the table. "Whoever labeled it morning sickness was wrong. I have it all day long. Yesterday I almost didn't make it through the ceremony. The smell of the flowers only made it worse."

Mia grabbed a sleeve of crackers from the cabinet. "Congratulations. Did Tony tell Sean? Because if he did, Sean didn't share the news." After hugging Cat, she joined her at the table.

"No. We decided not to say anything until after my brother and Ella's wedding. We didn't even tell our parents until after the reception last night. I'm sure it won't be long before half the town knows. They were all excited when we told them, especially my parents, since this will be their first grandchild."

Excited wasn't the word she'd use to describe Mom's reaction when she learned Mia and Sean were expecting. The word resigned summed it up much better. Angie didn't doubt it was because Sean was the father rather than someone like Anderson or Chad. Thankfully, by the time Natalie was born, Mom's feelings had changed, and while she might never be the same type of grandmother as Sean's mom, she loved Natalie.

What kind of reaction would Mom have if and when Angie became pregnant? The more time she spent with her niece, the more she realized she wanted children someday too. If her relationship with Dakota eventually led to marriage, would Mom treat him the same way she treated Sean? Never mind if they got married in the future. How would she treat him when she came to visit in October? Sean put up with it because he loved Mia. But would Dakota? Mia's statement aside, he'd never said he loved her.

Cat tore open the package of crackers. "Neither of you answered my question. Were you talking about Dakota?"

Mia nodded. "I think he loves her."

Cat took another sip of tea and pulled out a cracker. "Yeah, I agree. I have friends who would do almost anything to have their boyfriends look at them the way Dakota was looking at you."

"And I saw the glances you kept exchanging at the reception and this afternoon. I think you're half in love with him already." This time Mia's voice took on her "I'm your older sister and I know everything" tone. A tone she rarely used.

Both women focused their attention on her. She trusted Mia. Her sister would not repeat anything she said in this room. If Mia asked in Cat's presence, she must trust her; otherwise, she would've waited until they were alone again.

"Yes, and that's why I'm worried he'll have second thoughts after he has time to consider the media attention he's getting."

"I'm sure Dakota realized it would happen long before yesterday," Cat said.

Mia rolled her eyes. "See, I said the same thing. You have nothing to worry about."

Angie hoped her sister and Cat were right.

SIXTEEN

SHANE ACCEPTED the envelope containing all the signed paperwork from the real estate agent. Waiting for today had been excruciating, but finally, after several weeks, the house in Jefferson was his. The various legal documents in the manila envelope he held proved it.

"Welcome to New Hampshire," Teddy, one of the former owners of the home, said, extending his hand. "If you need anything, stop by my brother's house. Josh and his wife live next door to you."

"Thanks, I'll keep it in mind."

He didn't need anything. He'd planned everything out well in advance of this afternoon.

The same day he'd received a closing date from the bank, he'd put in for two weeks of vacation from work. He'd also arranged it so when he returned, he'd start working out of the Door2Door Express distribution center in Conway instead of the one in Danvers. Then he'd spent an entire weekend purchasing all the furniture they would need. At least for now. Once they had children, they would need additional items. Tomorrow they would deliver all of it to the house. He'd already packed everything he wanted to keep from his apartment. All he needed to do was pick up the van he'd rented to get it up here. A local charity always in need of items would pick up the furniture and other odds and ends he no longer wanted. On his lunch break yesterday, he'd stopped at the post office in North Salem and arranged to have all his mail forwarded to the post office box he'd rented in Jefferson. Finally, he made sure his shift at Masterson's last night was his final one.

"It's almost lunchtime. I usually treat my clients to either breakfast or lunch after a closing. Are you in a rush this after-noon?" Cathy asked, handing him the keys to his new house.

He appreciated all the help the real estate agent had given him, but he didn't want to spend any additional time with her today, even if it meant a free meal. He had a lot to do before he could bring Angie up. The sooner he got it done, the sooner they could be together every day and every night.

Shane put the house keys in his pocket. The real estate agent didn't need to know what his actual plans were for the day. "Unfortunately, I need to head straight back to North Salem so I'm not late for my shift at the restaurant. But thank you for all your help. You made the experience much easier than I was anticipating."

As intended, the compliment brought a smile to Cathy's face. "Well, if you have any questions, please just call me."

After leaving the office, he made a quick stop at the supermarket and picked up enough paper goods and food to last at least three weeks. He didn't want to bring Angie up to a house with no food in the freezer or toilet paper in the bath-room. Once they were settled and he knew what her favorite foods and beverages were, he'd stock up on them too. Since he had to go to work every day, he'd prefer not to waste any of their time together by making weekly trips to the store. In fact, he'd purchased a large freezer for the basement so he'd have the extra room to store everything from meat and frozen veggies to extra loaves of bread. Much like the furniture, the freezer was coming tomorrow.

The drive from the store to his house was a peaceful one. Unlike in North Salem, stop signs weren't around every turn, and he didn't have to worry about sharing the road with cyclists or people walking their dogs. Even better, there was no heavy traffic like he often encountered when he drove in and out of Boston or any of its neighboring cities.

From the outside, the log cabin looked much the way he remembered it. Even the wreath on the door and the flowers on the porch remained. The only things missing were the large wooden swing set, the green turtle-shaped sandbox, and the trampoline. Eventually, similar items would again fill the yard. He wanted his children to have the best of everything. Between the two of them, they'd make sure it happened when the time came.

Shane's hand shook, and it took him two attempts to get the door unlocked. Unlike on his first visit, the house was empty. The lack of furniture made the living room appear twice as large. Although the furniture was gone, the previous owners had left the curtains and window blinds. For now, those would do. When Angie moved in, she could order some she liked. When he entered the kitchen, he found a bottle of champagne and two wineglasses on the counter along with a card. After setting down the bags he held, he picked up the card and read the message inside.

We hope you and your girlfriend are as happy here as we were. Teddy and Briana

When he first met with Cathy, he'd mentioned to her that his girlfriend would be living with him. She must have shared the information with the listing agent, who in turn told his clients.

It took several trips, but eventually Shane had his car unloaded and all the perishable items put away. Satisfied for the moment, he carried the air mattress he'd brought with him up to the master bedroom. It wouldn't be as comfortable as the bed arriving tomorrow, but it beat sleeping on the floor tonight.

Like downstairs, the blinds and curtains remained on the windows, but the ugly green area rug was no longer there. Before he inflated the mattress, he pulled the blinds up so he could see the view. The sight of the White Mountains in the distance topped any view Angie would get looking out her bedroom window in North Salem.

Turning, he glanced around the room. Instead of seeing an empty space, though, he saw the king-size four-poster bed he'd purchased against one wall with Angie in it naked and waiting for him. Instantly his body reacted. If a mere image could do that to him, he could only imagine what the real sight would do.

Soon. She'll be here soon.

ANGIE SLIPPED her arm around Dakota's waist Friday night as they followed Mia and Sean out of The Half Door. Tonight was only the third time her sister and brother-in-law had gone out and left Natalie at home with Sean's mom. Remarkably, they'd only checked their cell phones half a dozen times all night.

"I thought your only hidden talents were knitting and sewing?" she asked.

Except for Sean, who was more than happy to sit back and watch, they all went up on stage at least once to perform some karaoke. Of the three of them, Dakota was by far the best. While she and Mia selected more current hits, he'd gone with a classic Elvis song. When it came to karaoke, some people had real talent, some had a lot of courage, and the rest fell somewhere in the middle. To her delight and probably the surprise of everyone in the club, Dakota had real talent.

"I think my exact words were that I can knit and sew. We all have hidden talents."

"He's right," Sean called out from in front of them. "Dakota never said those were his only two talents."

"It was implied in his statement. Don't you agree, Mia?"

Her sister didn't hesitate to answer. "Completely." Mia glanced back at them. "You really do have a great voice. It almost sounded as if they were playing a recording of the song."

She rarely listened to songs older than she was, but even she'd heard songs recorded by the King, as people often called him, so she had a general idea of what they should sound like. "My sister's right. Can you move like him too?"

"You've seen the extent of my ability when it comes to dancing."

"That's too bad. I was thinking we could have a jumpsuit similar to the ones he wore made for you. Then you could wear it the next time we go to The Half Door and swivel your hips while you belt out some songs."

Dakota turned his head in her direction. The streetlights provided enough illumination so she could see his frown. "Sorry, that's one fantasy I can't fulfill for you." He slowed his pace and brought his lips within mere inches of her ear. "But I'll take care of any other fantasies you have."

A tidal wave of heat broke over her and her pulse skyrocketed. They'd been lovers for well over a month now, yet the mere thought of being with him still sent her over the edge. Shifting her hand from his waist, she moved it into his back pocket.

"Do you want to come back to our house?" Sean asked when they reached the parking lot around the corner.

Angie glanced at her watch. By the time they got back to town, it'd be almost eleven o'clock. Any other Friday night, the hour wouldn't bother her, but Dakota had to work tomorrow. One thing she'd learned since being with Dakota, working for the FBI wasn't your average nine-to-five, forty-hour-a-week job. Some days he went in around the same time the sun was coming up. Other days he didn't return until late in the evening. Then there were occasions when he had to work on the weekends. Tomorrow would be the second Saturday he had to work since they'd been together.

"Not tonight. I need to be in Everett at six tomorrow morning." Dakota unlocked the car and opened the door for her.

"If I don't see you before you leave, have a good vacation." Sean used his key fob to unlock his truck.

Tuesday morning they were flying to Aruba for the week. She was looking forward to the vacation more than she'd looked forward to one in a long time. In general, they spent much of their free time together. They'd even spent a weekend together at a bed-and-breakfast up near the White Mountain National Forest. Still, she couldn't wait to have a whole week in paradise alone with Dakota and no disruptions.

Before Sean and Mia walked over to his truck, Mia hugged her. "Are you still coming over tomorrow?"

As if she didn't spend enough time at Mia's house these days. Ever since the contractor started the renovations on her house, she spent most afternoons at Mia's house because trying to work on her current screenplay with all the noise was impossible. The first time she complained about it to her sister and brother-in-law, they offered her the use of one of the spare bedrooms. Since then it had become her office where she worked almost every day. Tomorrow she wouldn't be going over to work though. Gram and Pop were visiting, and she hadn't seen them in a few weeks.

"Yep. I'll be by sometime in the morning." Gram and Pop said they would be there around noon. She wanted to get as much time as she could with Natalie before they arrived. Once her grandparents got there, they'd monopolize her niece.

"See you then," Mia replied before they walked over to Sean's truck.

Dakota waited until she was in the car before walking around to the other side. It wasn't something he did all the time, and she wouldn't want him to except when they were in a parking lot late at night.

Angie waited to speak until they'd turned onto the street. "I wasn't joking before. You really do have a great voice."

"My mom used to say the same thing. She wanted me to join the chorus in high school. It interfered with sports too much. Even if it hadn't, I don't think I would've done it." He kept both eyes on the road but reached for her left hand. "If I didn't have to leave so early in the morning, I'd suggest you spend the night."

Over the past two weeks or so, they'd spent more nights together than they did apart. Even though they each had keys to the other's house, they spent more time at his place because of the mess at hers. And since she spent so many nights with him, she'd left some clothes as well as some toiletries there. Once the renovations were complete, she was going to suggest he do the same at her house.

She didn't mind waking up early. She didn't tell him, though, because then he might ask her to stay. Unfortunately, she wouldn't have the willpower to say no, which meant he wouldn't get the sleep he needed because when they got into bed, falling asleep would be the furthest thing from either of their minds.

"If all goes as planned, I should be home around two tomorrow, so we should have plenty of time to get to the game."

She'd enjoyed the first baseball game they went to so much that she purchased them tickets to this weekend's game against New York. Everyone she talked to insisted there was nothing quite like a baseball game between New York and Boston.

"I'll still be at Mia's. If you pick me up there, you can meet Gram and Pop."

Other than Avery and of course Mia, Dakota had met none of her family members yet. Although she was less than excited about him meeting Mom in October, she wanted him to get to know her grandparents, as well as her dad. And especially Gram wanted to meet him. During her most recent visit to Woodlawn, one of Gram's first questions had been whether or not she had someone special in her life. While she'd left out the more intimate details, she'd filled Gram in on her relationship with Dakota.

They passed the sign welcoming them to North Salem, and Dakota switched on the car's high beams. Only a few roads in town had streetlights, and the heavy fog tonight made the visibility low.

"After I stop home and shower, I'll be over. And if something comes up and I'm running late, I'll let you know." He turned onto her street. Except for one, all the houses were in darkness. She'd noticed most of her neighbors went to bed early even on the weekends.

The sensor lights on the garage lit up the entire driveway and part of the front yard. Regardless, Dakota walked her inside.

"Be careful."

He insisted the arrests he would be taking part in tomorrow were nothing like what she saw in the movies, and that everyone involved did everything to make them as safe as possible. He'd even given her the exact number of FBI agents who had been killed while in the line of duty. She couldn't deny the number was remarkably low, but it didn't stop her from worrying about him. Maybe as time went on, the fear would diminish, but tomorrow's arrests would be his first since they'd become so close.

His arms encircled her and held her snugly against his body. "You've got nothing to worry about. Promise." He lowered his mouth to hers and kissed her with such tenderness she shivered. His kiss didn't stay tender. Soon her heart hammered in her chest, and she yanked his shirt from his waistband so she could slide her hands along his bare skin.

Without any warning Dakota's lips left hers. "If I don't stop, I'll never leave."

She felt the rapid rise and fall of his chest against hers as well as his erection pressing against her.

"I'll be over as soon as I can tomorrow." He released her and took a step back.

"Be—"

"Stop worrying."

Irrational or not, her concern was real.

"I love you." For weeks now she'd known she loved him. And she truly believed he felt the same way, even though he hadn't spoken the words either. Blurting the truth out tonight hadn't crossed her mind once, but if he was going into a potentially dangerous situation, she needed him to know how she felt.

He gifted her with the very smile that had caught her attention the first time they met. It no longer momentarily left her speechless but caused her internal temperature to jump a notch.

Slipping his hands up her arms, he brought her in close again. "And I love you."

She couldn't let the declaration go without at least a quick kiss, so she brushed her lips against his before moving away. "See you tomorrow afternoon."

SEVENTEEN

BY THREE O'CLOCK MONDAY AFTERNOON, she was almost all packed for their trip, and as far as she was concerned, that was good enough for now. It wasn't like she couldn't finish with Dakota here. What she couldn't do with him here was work on her screenplay, and she certainly wouldn't be able to do it when they were in Aruba.

The house was quiet for a change. The contractor and his assistants had left for the day over an hour ago, and they wouldn't be back until she returned from vacation. When the contractor dropped the news on her last week, it had annoyed her. She was well past anxious to get the kitchen and back staircase in working order again. Unfortunately, the rest of the cabinets and flooring she'd selected wouldn't be delivered until next week, and since the master bathroom was complete, there wasn't much more they could do until the materials came in. Dakota suggested it was a good thing the men wouldn't be around this week. While she didn't stay home the entire time they were there, she always let them in when they arrived and returned before they left. If they worked while she was in Aruba, she'd have to either give them a house key or ask Mia to come over in the morning to let them in and return later to lock up. Neither option appealed to her.

Before they'd started on the kitchen, she'd gotten in the habit of using the back staircase since it was closer to her bedroom. With the stairs temporarily gone, she grabbed her cell phone off the nightstand and walked down the hallway. When she originally decided to remodel, replacing the old servants' stairs hadn't entered her mind. Gregg had incorporated the additional facelift into his designs for the kitchen, and she'd been unable to disagree that what he had in mind would look much better than what was there now. So she'd given him the go-ahead, increasing the amount of time and money it would take to complete the project.

When she came home earlier, she'd left her laptop in the library. On the occasions she did any writing at home these days, she worked in there. The bookshelves held both her favorite novels as well as her many books on writing, character development, and grammar. In a few months, when the cooler temperatures moved in, she pictured herself working in there while a fire crackled in the fireplace and she had a cup of hot chocolate nearby. For now, she'd have to settle for working with the windows open so she could enjoy the fresh air while a bottle of water sat on her desk.

Opening the file containing her current work in process, Angie allowed her creative side to take over and lost herself in the story.

The ringing cell phone near her laptop pulled her back to reality two hours later, and it couldn't have been at a worse time. She'd been struggling with this scene for days. In fact, she'd skipped it entirely yesterday, hoping if she took some time away from it, she'd figure out exactly how it should play out. Her plan worked. Not long after she started writing, the entire scene fell into place for her. She had more than half of it written, and she wanted it finished before Dakota arrived and she didn't touch the laptop again for several days.

She glanced at the device to see whom the call was from before picking it up and answering. She made the mistake of answering a call yesterday from a number not in her contact list. It had turned out to be an individual doing a survey about the upcoming election.

"I'm running behind," Dakota explained after they exchanged greetings. "The traffic on 128 was worse than usual. I need a quick shower before I do anything else. It was hot at the range today. I'll be over as soon as I'm done."

Once a quarter, all agents had to pass a firearms qualification test. Dakota had done his today, so instead of being in an air-conditioned office building all day, he'd been outside at the firing range.

They'd agreed he'd pick her up after work and they'd stay at his house tonight. She could just as easily drive over to his house instead and leave her car in his garage for the week. "Do you—" The doorbell stopped her midsentence. "I'll be right back. There's someone at the door. It's probably something I ordered."

Leaving the cell phone on the desk, she pushed her chair back. She'd recently ordered all the bedding, curtains, and lamps for the spare bedroom her parents would use when they came next month. She'd expected the order to arrive last week. On Wednesday, however, she received an email from the company explaining two of the items were temporally out of stock, and the order wouldn't arrive until sometime this week.

The doorbell rang a second time before she reached the foyer. "Hold your horses. I'm coming."

Opening the door, she found Shane from Door2Door Express on the steps holding a large package in his hands.

"I was hoping my order would come before I left." She didn't want packages sitting outside her house while she was away, and her sister had more important things to do than come by to see if it was there.

"It's heavy. Where would you like it?"

If he left it near the door, she could unpack it and carry the items up or ask Dakota to bring it to the bedroom for her later. "Right here's fine." She pointed to a spot near the door and moved back so he could enter.

If the box was heavy, it didn't appear as though Shane was struggling with it when he walked inside and placed it where she indicated.

"Thank you."

"Anytime." He turned as if to leave, but instead he pushed the front door closed. "And now that we'll be together every day, I can take care of you all the time."

Angie didn't stop to consider where she'd go once she got out of the house. She just needed to get away from Shane. Rushing forward, she tried to reach the door.

Shane moved immediately, blocking her escape. "The house is ready. I wanted everything perfect before we moved in, but if there's something you don't like, you can change it. And wait until you see the view from our bedroom window. It's breathtaking."

The last time he delivered a package, something about him made her uncomfortable. Later she'd told herself she was being silly, that he was harmless. She'd never been more wrong in her life. The guy was crazy. Not only that, he was a lot bigger than her. No one would call her short, but Shane was at least four inches taller and muscular. She'd never be able to fight him off.

"I can't wait to show you." He reached out for her hand, but she clasped them behind her back before he touched her.

"It'll take us a few hours to get home, but I have sandwiches in the car for us."

Her neighbors could probably hear her heart, it was beating so hard. "I can't go tonight." It was a long shot, but maybe she could get him to leave if he thought she'd go with him another time. "I promised to babysit my niece. We can go tomorrow instead."

Angie moved farther away from him. She doubted she could outrun him, but if she made it to the kitchen, she might be able to go out the back door and at least try.

She only managed a few steps before Shane followed her.

"We've been apart long enough. She'll have to find another babysitter." Reaching toward his waist, he removed the gun he had holstered under his shirt. "It's time to go, Angie."

The chances of her outrunning him were low, but the possibility of her outrunning a bullet was nonexistent. And she didn't need to take another step closer to the kitchen to know he'd follow her if she did.

If she had her phone, maybe she could somehow dial 911, but it was…. Her thoughts came to a standstill. Dakota was still on the phone waiting for her to finish their conversation. If she went in the other room, maybe she could say something and Dakota would overhear. If he suspected something was wrong, he'd call the police.

Looked like it was time to play the biggest role of her life.

Smiling, she touched Shane's shoulder. "You're right, Mia can ask Maureen to babysit. But there are some things I need to take with me. My laptop is in the other room." She headed toward the library.

Since she was cooperating, she waited for him to put the gun away.

He didn't. But at least he didn't follow her into the room either. Instead, he remained near the doorway watching her.

"I've been working on this screenplay for about a month. It's coming along. If you want, I'll let you read what I have so far when we get home tonight."

Could Dakota hear her? She didn't dare touch the cell phone, but she glanced at the screen. The connection was still open. Dakota hadn't hung up. But was her voice loud enough?

Her hands shook as she closed the laptop and unplugged it. "It won't take me long to pack some clothes, Shane." Tucking the device into her backpack, she glanced at her cell phone again. If Dakota heard her, he hadn't disconnected yet to call the police.

"Don't worry about packing a lot. I'll buy you whatever you need."

He wasn't as close to the cell phone as her, but hopefully, Dakota could hear Shane's voice as well.

Angie left the backpack on the desk on top of her cell phone. If the police didn't get here before Shane forced her out the door, maybe she could somehow slip the device into the bag later. She certainly couldn't do it now with him watching her.

She touched his arm as she passed by him into the hall. "I'll be right back." *Please don't follow me.*

Once she reached the top of the stairs, she jogged down the hallway and straight to the master bedroom. None of the rooms had locks on the doors. She hadn't seen the need to have any installed since she lived alone. Angie wished she had one on her bedroom door now. It might not stop Shane from dragging her out of the house, but it would slow him down.

Crossing the room, she looked out the window. She couldn't tell the exact distance to the ground, but it looked like a lot. There was nothing under the window to break her fall either. If she jumped, she'd probably break a leg or an ankle when she hit the ground. She wouldn't be able to run if she broke either. She'd be a sitting duck waiting for Shane to find her and drag her off.

If the back staircase was still in place, she could slip down those and be out the kitchen door before he realized she was gone, but all the treads were missing, making it useless.

Dakota heard me. He'll call the police. Somehow she just needed to make sure Shane didn't get her out of the house before help came.

The attic. She could hide up there. Only a handful of people knew the secret room existed, and Shane wasn't one of them.

DAKOTA FINISHED his bottle of water and tossed it in the trash. What was taking Angie so long to come back? He could've taken his shower and been half dressed by now. After he removed his hat, he kicked off his shoes. The temperature today had been in the high 90s with 100 percent humidity, making for an unpleasant day at the range. All his clothes were soaked with sweat. Hell, even his baseball hat was sweaty.

"I've been working on this screenplay for about a month. It's coming along. If you want, I'll let you read what I have so far when we get home tonight." The sound of Angie's voice came through his phone, but she wasn't talking to him. Not only wouldn't she be telling him that because he already knew, but if she'd been talking into her phone, her voice would be much louder.

She'd gotten friendly with Ella and Cat over the past few weeks, but he doubted either would stop at this hour on a Monday night.

"It won't take me long to pack some clothes, Shane."

His entire body froze as a giant hand reached into his chest and squeezed. Dakota didn't know who Shane was, but there was no mistaking the desperation and fear in Angie's voice.

"Don't worry about packing a lot. I'll buy you whatever you need." Shane's voice was softer, indicating he was farther from wherever Angie's cell phone was.

Dakota shoved his shoes on and raced down the stairs. Most days he found it a nuisance that he carried two phones, one for work calls and another for personal ones. At the moment, having two meant he could keep the connection with Angie's phone and call the police.

Afraid of alerting whoever was in the house to his arrival, he parked in front of a house several feet away. A maroon-colored two-door car was parked in Angie's driveway. It was the only indication something was wrong.

The fear squeezing his heart urged him to knock down the door and rush inside. His common sense and years with the FBI told him to hold back and wait for the police to arrive. Going into an unknown situation alone was a terrible idea, and at the moment, he had few details about the situation inside. Nothing Angie said let him know if the guy had a weapon or not. He also had no way of knowing where in the house they were. When she went upstairs to pack, had Shane followed her? If he hadn't, there were plenty of rooms on the first floor for the guy to wait in. The only one he might not bother with was the kitchen. The room had no furniture or even counters.

When he'd called her earlier, she'd been in the library working. If she'd left her phone in there while she answered the door, she couldn't have been far from the room when he heard her talking. Maybe the asshole inside had stayed in there while Angie went up to pack. There was no way to tell.

Not another sound had come through the phone since Shane told her she didn't need to pack a lot.

The police should be there at any moment. But he couldn't wait. Already the guy had been in there long enough to do God knew what. He needed to get her out of the house now.

Dakota paused long enough to grab both his cell phones off the passenger seat. Then he sprinted toward Angie's neighbor. Since he didn't know where Shane was, he figured his best point of entry would be through the kitchen door. He kept his fingers crossed that no one would be in the Plantes' backyard when he jogged through it toward Angie's house. He didn't have the time to answer their questions, and he didn't need them interfering.

Drawing his gun, he unlocked the door and quietly slipped inside.

"Do you need help, Angie?" a male voice inside the house called out.

He didn't know Shane's exact location, but he was on this floor. Dakota listened for Angie's response as he crept across the kitchen. He wanted her as far away from danger as possible, considering the situation.

"Angie?" Shane called out again when she didn't reply.

Unless she jumped out a window, there was no way for her to escape the second floor. She had to be in the house. Was she hiding, hoping to delay the asshole's plans until help got there? If she was hiding, someone in Shane's state of mind would be pissed when they found her. There was no way to know what he might do once he got angry.

He couldn't let Shane get upstairs.

With his weapon at the ready, he silently moved down toward the library.

Dakota recognized the guy moving away from the sofa.

He'd seen him waiting tables at Masterson's restaurant. Something about the guy had always struck him as a little odd when he waited on him, but nothing suggested he was out of his mind.

More importantly, he recognized the make and model of the gun sitting on the table next to the sofa. Before Shane saw it, Dakota moved his pistol behind his right leg so it wouldn't be visible but still ready in case he needed it. If left with no other choice, he'd do it, but he'd rather not shoot someone in Angie's house.

Shane's eyebrows bunched together and he blinked rapidly when he spotted Dakota, then he took one step back toward the sofa and end table.

"You don't want to do that." Dakota kept his left hand up and facing Shane while at the same time keeping his body slightly angled with his gun still hidden behind his leg.

He stopped. "I'm not going to let you stop us." His nostrils flared as he formed a fist. "Angie loves me. We belong together. I have everything ready for her."

"I know she does." Dakota struggled to keep his tone neutral. He wanted to end this in the safest way possible, which meant he had to talk this guy down, keep him from picking up his weapon. As soon as Shane reached for his gun, Dakota would have no choice but to shoot him. "I'm here to help you."

Shane's gaze drifted past Dakota toward the foyer for a brief moment before settling on his face again.

Angie, please stay upstairs. He moved farther into the room. "There are things you need to do before you and Angie can be together."

"I don't need help. I know how to make Angie happy."

"Then you've already spoken with her father? She comes from a very traditional family. It's important to her that you get Dominic's blessing. If you don't, she'll never be truly happy." Dakota took another step closer. "What about a ring? She doesn't just want to live with you, she wants to get married."

Shane glanced in the direction of the end table before glaring at Dakota again. "How the hell would you know what'll make her happy?"

"We've been friends since we were kids. Except for you, no one knows her better than I do. C'mon, let's go over to Masterson's. We can have a beer and make sure you've done everything you need to." He nodded toward the front door. "Let me help you, Shane."

Sweat trickled down his temple, but he ignored it as he waited for Shane's answer while at the same time listening for any sign the police had arrived. The last thing he wanted was for them to announce their presence. He almost had Shane. If the guy learned the police were outside waiting for him, he might lunge for his gun. Once he did that, it would be all over for him.

Shane nodded.

Every muscle in Dakota's body tensed. He only had one chance at this.

Dakota allowed Shane to exit the room first and followed him out the door. They made it down the front steps before the police converged on them.

More than anything, he wanted to locate Angie, make sure she was okay and let her know she was safe. Instead, he waited to see the police slip handcuffs on Shane and for Captain Ellsbury to reach him.

"His gun is on a table in the library." The police would want to collect it as evidence. "I know you'll need a statement from me, but first I need to find Angie." Rather than stick around for a response, he sprinted into the house and up the staircase.

"Angie." He paused at the top of the stairs and waited. When all he got was silence, he walked into the last bedroom on the right. Today the bookcase wasn't as flush against the wall as the first time she showed him the room. When designed, the owners had most likely assumed someone in the bedroom would be closing the secret entrance, not the person on the other side, making it hard for Angie to close the door. Still, it was good enough that a person could walk by the bookcase a dozen times and not know what was behind it.

HUDDLED ON THE FLOOR, Angie pulled her knees in closer to her chest. Until today, she'd never minded the dark. After this she might carry a flashlight around with her all the time.

Assuming I get out of here. Left with no way to escape the house, hiding in the attic seemed like a far better idea than trying to come up with excuses for why they couldn't leave until the police got there. After sitting in the dark, she was having second thoughts.

What if Dakota hadn't heard her conversation with Shane? Maybe he thought she hadn't come back to the phone because she'd injured herself. If he didn't know Shane was in the house, he might walk in and find Shane's pistol pointed at his chest. Up here she couldn't hear or see anything, but a gunshot was loud. If Shane did shoot Dakota, she'd probably hear it. And it would be her fault.

An image of Dakota flat on the floor staring at the ceiling while blood pooled around him materialized. The gruesome image turned her blood to ice, and she shivered.

Forcing it away, she reminded herself there was another possibility.

Dakota might have heard what she said to Shane before coming upstairs. He might be outside right now helping the police come up with a plan. There were no windows up here, so she couldn't peek out and see what was happening.

On top of all that, it didn't help that Angie had no idea how long she'd been up there. She didn't have a watch on, so ten minutes or five hours could've passed since she climbed the ladder.

A sliver of light broke the inky darkness. Slowly it grew. The ladder creaked as someone started up it, and Angie clenched her fists. She'd had a little trouble getting the door closed. Had Shane noticed it and decided to investigate? If it was Shane, she wasn't going to leave with him without putting up a fight.

"Angie."

At the sound of Dakota's voice, she closed her eyes and took a deep breath, then scrambled out of the corner she'd backed herself into. "In here."

The door didn't allow in much light, but it was enough to see Dakota looked unharmed as he reached the top of the ladder. "Are you okay?"

"I should be asking you that."

He entered the small room, taking up the rest of the space. She winced at the sound of his head making contact with the low ceiling before sitting down. If it hurt, it didn't stop Dakota from wrapping his arms around her and pulling her onto his lap.

"Are you okay?" His eyes searched her face. Even in the dim light, she saw the concern lurking in them.

Nodding, Angie wrapped her arms around him as she started to shake. She'd managed to hold it together until this point. Now that she was safe in Dakota's arms, her body was buckling under the stress.

"You're shivering. Are you sure you're not hurt?" The concern she saw in his eyes echoed in his voice as he tightened his arms around her.

"Honest, I'm fine. He didn't touch me." She pulled back, forcing him to loosen his embrace. No longer plastered against his body, she kissed him. "You never answered me. How are you?"

"I just had ten years shaved off my life, but otherwise I'm fine."

She didn't need to ask for clarification. She understood the meaning behind his statement. "Where's Shane?" She didn't want him to ever be able to do what he'd done today again. At the same time, she didn't want him dead on her library floor either.

"I handed him off to the police."

She'd believed once Dakota figured out something was wrong, he'd call the police and either assist them in some manner or let them handle the situation. It didn't sound like that was what happened. "Didn't you call the police before coming over?"

"I did, but when I got here, they hadn't arrived. So I did what I needed to do. Every second you were in here alone with that guy was a second too long."

The sudden burst of anger surprised her. "He had a gun. He could've killed you." The image of Dakota's lifeless body on the floor returned. "You should've waited for the police."

"I couldn't wait. Not when you were in danger."

His words melted away her anger. If their positions had been reversed, she would've done anything within her power to protect him. "You should've at least put on your body armor." She'd never seen him wearing it, but she knew he had some. She'd even asked him to show it to her last week.

"The police need to speak with you. Are you ready to go downstairs?"

"Is Shane still out there?" She could handle talking to the police, but she didn't want to see Shane again.

Dakota pressed a kiss against her forehead. "I don't know

if they've taken him away yet, but the police will come inside to talk to you. If you're not ready, you can stay here a few more minutes, but I need to go down and tell them you're safe."

She'd spent more than enough time alone in the tiny room. "The sooner I do it, the sooner it'll be over." Angie hugged him again, both to reassure herself he was okay and to express her feelings. "Thank you." The two words seemed insufficient. He'd saved her from being kidnapped. If not for Dakota, she'd be with Shane right now, off to whatever destination he had planned for them.

"No thank-you required. I'll be here whenever you need me."

Angie disagreed, but she wasn't going to argue with him. Moving off his lap, she started down the ladder.

There were several police officers downstairs, and she could see the patrol cars parked outside. Her neighbors must be wondering what was going on. Of course, it wouldn't be long before the whole town knew what happened.

She paused at the bottom of the stairs. She needed to call Mia as soon as possible. The last thing she wanted was for her sister to hear about what happened from someone else. But that conversation would need to wait, because Captain Ellsbury, whom she'd met at her sister's wedding, was approaching her.

The captain gestured toward the door after they exchanged a greeting. "The paramedics are here to check you out and bring you to the ER if necessary."

"I'm okay. He didn't hurt me." At least he didn't hurt her physically; emotionally was another story. She might be safe, but her emotions were still on a roller coaster. She expected them to be that way for a long time.

Relief spread across Captain Ellsbury's face. "I'm glad to

hear it. If you're up to it, we do need to get a statement from you."

Her stomach roiled at the mere thought of detailing the events of the afternoon. Angie nodded and swallowed the excessive saliva pooling in her mouth. "I'll tell you whatever you need to know."

EPILOGUE

Two months later

ANGIE WATCHED the fire burning in the fireplace while she listened to her sister. An unusually early snowstorm had dropped three inches of snow on the area yesterday. She'd taken that to be Mother Nature's hint it was cold enough to light a fire in the fireplace. Thanks to Dakota's lesson when they went camping back in September, she'd managed to get it going on her first try. She'd been in the library ever since, writing.

She'd hoped to be further along with the project by now, but setbacks kept popping up. The first had been her parents' unexpected visit in September following the kidnapping attempt. Dad had accepted her reassurance that she was fine. Mom, on the other hand, had insisted she move back to her Los Angeles home in its gated community. They'd had multiple heated arguments about it during the three days her parents were in town. Then it seemed no sooner had they left than they were back in October for their planned visit. While Mom stopped pestering her about moving because North Salem wasn't safe, she constantly complained about every other decision she'd made in the past few months, including her relationship with Dakota.

She'd spent enough time listening to Mom's views of Sean that she'd anticipated her attitude when she met Dakota. Mom hadn't disappointed. It didn't seem to matter that Dakota had risked his life to save her. In Mom's eyes, he was wrong for her. According to her, Angie needed someone who could enhance her career and who knew how to handle media attention. Dad hadn't shared his wife's views, which didn't surprise Angie. Her parents often disagreed. Sometimes she wondered how they'd remained married after all these years.

Avery, on the other hand, had surprised her.

In the beginning, her sister had been dead set against Angie's move and, to some extent, her involvement with Dakota. Over the past two months, Avery's opinion had changed. She no longer pestered Angie about taking new roles. When her sister did call, they discussed every other topic under the sun, but work never entered their conversations. Perhaps even more surprising was the number of visits Avery had made to town since Angie's move. Angie wasn't sure of the exact number because she'd stopped counting after her sister's sixth trip.

"You are not." Angie reached for her hot chocolate and waited for Avery's reply.

"I'm serious."

Avery sounded sincere, but Angie wasn't buying it. "You hate it here." Maybe hate was a strong word, but North Salem wasn't her sister's favorite place either.

"I never said I hated it. I just didn't understand what you loved about it so much. But it's grown on me. Trust me, I'm not going to live there all year round. You know I hate the snow. But since you, Mia, and Natalie are all there, I plan on being around more and want a place of my own."

Her eldest sister had fallen in love with their niece as quickly as she had. "Do you want to rent or buy?"

"Not sure. I guess I'm open to either. But I don't want anything old. You and Mia can keep your historic houses. I want something built in this century. "

She sipped her drink. Already she knew the perfect place for her sister. Before she could suggest it, she had one other person to talk to. "There's a nice house not far from me. I think it'll be available soon. I'll let you know."

Their conversation moved away from Avery's interest in getting a house and to what they'd both already purchased their niece for Christmas, which was quickly approaching.

"I'll call you tomorrow," Angie said when she heard the front door open.

Rarely did they spend a night apart. In fact, since the kidnapping attempt, they'd spent only eight nights apart, and three of those had been when Dakota traveled to Florida for work. They'd spent most nights at Dakota's house while the contractor finished the kitchen and back stairs. These days they spent two or three nights at his house and the rest of the week here. She didn't mind staying at his house, but in her opinion it was silly for them to be constantly going back and forth. And she had a plan for putting an end to it. She'd just been waiting for a good time to suggest it. Today seemed as good a day any.

The scent of tomato sauce wafted in the room before Dakota. The monthly poker game was tonight, and she'd offered to host. Before he left for work, he promised to pick food up on the way home. He knew her plan was to write all day, and once she got going, she often lost track of time. In fact, if Avery hadn't called and disturbed her, she'd still probably be typing away.

Leaning toward her, Dakota brushed his lips against hers. Although they usually weren't pulse-altering kisses, every morning before Dakota left and every night when he came home, he kissed her. "Still working?"

"Nope. I was talking to Avery." She pointed toward the bags. "Something smells good."

"Pizzas and an order of bruschetta from Tuscany. And before you ask, yes, I remembered an order of the calamari."

The calamari served at Tuscany, the Italian restaurant in town, was her favorite dish on their menu. It was possible she'd eat all of it before their friends arrived for the game.

"I knew I loved you for a reason."

Following him into the kitchen, she waited for him to notice the cake on the counter. Thanks to her sister and Maureen, she'd learned her way around the kitchen enough that she'd never starve. Today, she'd decided to challenge herself before sitting down to write. The three-tier vanilla cake with homemade buttercream frosting and raspberry filling was the end result.

After putting the pizzas in the oven to keep them warm, Dakota pointed toward the cake. "Is this to share tonight, or can I try some now?"

"You'll need to wait. But there is some leftover frosting in the fridge if you want to sample some." Ice cream might be his biggest weakness, but he never turned down anything sweet.

He didn't hesitate to grab the plastic container and dip a spoon inside it. Rather than lick it off, he swiped his finger through the sugar concoction. Before she could ask what he was up to, he spread it on her lips and kissed her.

Unlike in the library, he took his time teasing her lips

before touching his tongue to hers. Once inside, he set about making love to her mouth while setting a fire in her blood.

DAKOTA SLID his palms beneath the fabric of her leggings and pulled her closer to him. At the moment he wanted nothing more than to strip her clothes off and make love to her. He was debating whether to start undressing her in here or wait until they were in the bedroom. Before he could make up his mind, Angie's hands closed around his wrists and she pulled his hands free.

"We don't have time." Her voice simmered with the same desire racing through his body.

Freeing his arm, he slipped her top off her shoulder and kissed her bare skin. "Not even if we're quick?"

"Right, like that'll ever happen." She gave him a gentle push and pulled her shirt back into place.

She had a point. When they made love, it was never quick. He enjoyed pleasing her too much to rush. The same was true on her part.

"Then I hope everyone loses their money and leaves early tonight." In the meantime, he'd have to deal with the discomfort he was currently in. "Do you want to set things up in the dining room or in here?"

Either room was large enough to hold everyone, and both were fully furnished.

"In the dining room. I thought we could use the fireplace."

Dakota grabbed a beer from the refrigerator and popped it open. Although she enjoyed the blood orange sour brewed at a local brewery, she wasn't a huge beer drinker. She preferred wine or fruity mixed drinks, but she always kept some of his favorite beers around. In return he made sure plenty of her favorite beverages and foods were in his kitchen. "Tell me what you need me to do."

"I'm not sure we need to do much. I already left plates and utensils on the buffet. We should be able to fit all the food on it too. And the cards and poker chips are in the dining room. There are plenty of chairs in there, so we don't need to move any from in here."

Sounded like she had everything under control. "Do you want a quick refresher?" Unless she'd been playing against the computer, she hadn't touched a deck of cards since last month's poker game. While she had fun, or at least she said she did, Angie hadn't won a single hand.

"Nah, if I lose, I lose. It's just for fun."

It was her money. If she wanted to hand it all over to Tony or Sean, it was her business. Pulling out a chair, he sat at the table. "How's Avery? Is she planning another visit soon?"

In the beginning, he'd been apprehensive about her eldest sister. Especially after the conversation they had at Sean's house when the pictures of Angie and him first hit the media. Either he'd misjudged her, or Avery's attitude had changed, because over the past couple months, a good relationship had developed between them. When she came to town, their interactions were easygoing and friendly—the complete opposite of the two times Angie's mom had been in town.

Before Lynn's first visit, he'd assumed Sean was exaggerating a little when he talked about his mother-in-law. He'd started to reconsider his view when she and Dominic came immediately after the kidnapping attempt. But even then he'd told himself the stressful situation was somehow affecting Lynn's personality and bringing out the worst in her. After her second visit in October, he understood why his friend couldn't stand to be in the same room with the woman. She simply was an unpleasant individual who not only believed she was better than everyone else but felt she knew what was best for her daughters. And when they didn't do as she wished, she did everything she could to change their minds.

How Angie's father stayed with the woman was a mystery. He hadn't spent as much time around Dominic. Unlike his wife, when they'd returned to North Salem in October, he'd stayed only a week before returning to California. Dakota had more than one conversation with the man, and he'd seen him interact with Angie, Mia, and Sean. At least during that week, he'd come across as a down-to-earth man who cared more about his daughters' happiness than their career decisions.

"She's good. She'll be here for Thanksgiving next week." She finished pouring a glass of wine and joined him. "Actually, she wants to either buy a house or rent one in town."

Dakota choked on the beer he'd swallowed. "She wants to move here?"

With a chuckle, she nodded. "I had a similar reaction. She doesn't want to make this her permanent home, but she wants her own place."

"Unless she's spending months at a time in town, wouldn't it be easier to either stay with either you or Mia? Maybe check into the Victorian Rose?"

Angie sipped her drink before answering. "Avery said she plans on being around a lot more, which I interpret to mean she intends to make her visits a couple of months long rather than a week or two. According to her, it's because Mia, Natalie, and I are here, and I'm sure it's a big factor, but I think there's another reason she plans to visit more."

If it was to get away from her mother, he understood Avery's desire to spend several months living in North Salem. Hell, if he were in her shoes, he'd consider living in Antarctica several months of the year rather than be close to Lynn Troy.

"Between you and me, I think she wants to see where things with Steve will go."

"Steve? What am I missing" As far as he knew, Avery and Steve, at least the only Steve he knew, had gone out once and only once back in August.

"Since August, every time she's around, they've gotten together. When she's not here, they stay in contact."

He now knew how Alice felt when she fell down the rabbit hole. "Steve Nelson, Sean's friend? The one who owns the karate school?"

"Uh, I thought I told you. Anyway, yes, Sean's friend."

Well, if Avery was serious, maybe she could either rent his house or Angie's. At this point they were living together and splitting up the time they spent at each house. In no way did it make financial sense for them to keep doing that.

"I told her I might know of the perfect place." Angie glanced down at her watch before lacing her fingers with his. "Almost every night I either stay at your house or you're here. It's silly for us each to have a house. I'd love it if you'd move in here with me."

For weeks he'd been wondering about the right time to bring up the topic. She'd beat him to it. Maybe he should've expected that. After all, she'd been the one to ask him out on their first date. From now on, he'd better stay on his toes, or she'd ask him to marry her before he managed to do it. Exactly when it would happen, he didn't know for certain, but he had started searching for a ring.

"If you like your house better, I can move in with you."

He liked his house, but he loved Angie's. It had character.

"But if you want to wait a little longer, we can keep doing things the way we have been," she added before he could get a single word out.

Before she continued, he touched his index finger to her

lips. "Tell Avery she can rent my house for as long as she wants. I don't need it."

I HOPE you enjoyed Dakota and Angie's story. If you want to spend more time in North Salem, check out The Billionaire Playboy and The Billionaire's Homecoming. Both books take place in North Salem.

ABOUT CHRISTINA

USA Today Best Selling author, Christina Tetreault started writing at the age of 10 on her grandmother's manual type-writer and never stopped. Born and raised in Lincoln, Rhode Island, she has lived in four of the six New England states since getting married in 2001. Today, she lives in New Hampshire with her husband, three daughters and two dogs. When she's not driving her daughters around or chasing around the dogs, she is working on a story or reading a romance novel. Currently, she has three series out, The Sherbrookes of Newport, Love on The North Shore and Elite Force Security. You can visit her website www.christinatetreault.com or follow her on Facebook to learn more about her characters and to track her progress on current writing projects.

Printed in Great Britain
by Amazon